WILD WHEELS

"Those guys who attacked Johnny today just gave us the slip," Nancy told Frank and Joe. "I also think—"

The rest of her sentence was drowned out by the sudden roar of a powerful engine. From a darkened doorway across the courtyard, a motorcycle shot out of its hiding place.

Frank ran to intercept it, but his foot slipped on the uneven cobblestones. Nancy watched as his feet flew up and he slammed down hard.

The engine was gunned as the cycle changed course and headed in Frank's direction.

The driver had taken dead aim at Frank, and Nancy and Joe were too far away to get to him in time!

NANCY DREW AND THE HARDY BOYS
TEAM UP
IN A SIZZLING SUPERMYSTERY

Nancy Drew & Hardy Boys SuperMysteries

Available from ARCHWAY Paperbacks

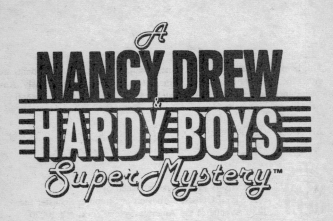

A NANCY DREW & HARDY BOYS Super Mystery™

THE PARIS CONNECTION

Carolyn Keene

AN ARCHWAY PAPERBACK
Published by POCKET BOOKS
New York   London   Toronto   Sydney   Tokyo   Singapore

AN ARCHWAY PAPERBACK *Original*

An Archway Paperback published by
POCKET BOOKS, a division of Simon & Schuster Inc.
1230 Avenue of the Americas, New York, NY 10020

Copyright © 1990 by Simon & Schuster Inc.
Cover art copyright © 1990 James Mathewuse
Produced by Mega-Books of New York, Inc

ISBN: 0-671-74675-8

First Archway Paperback printing April 1990

10 9 8   7   6   5   4

NANCY DREW, THE HARDY BOYS. AN ARCHWAY PAPERBACK and colophon are registered trademarks of Simon & Schuster Inc.

NANCY DREW & HARDY BOYS SUPERMYSTERY
is a trademark of Simon & Schuster Inc.

Printed in the U.S.A.

IL 6+

Chapter

One

BESS MARVIN looked around the crowd in the airport arrival area with wonder in her sparkling blue eyes. "Now I *know* we're in Paris!" she exclaimed, grabbing her friend Nancy Drew's arm. "I just heard a little boy speaking perfect French, and he couldn't have been more than three years old!"

Nancy laughed. Then she shifted the strap of her leather carry-on bag and brushed a strand of reddish blond hair from her face. "Last I heard, Bess, all French kids speak French."

Bess shot Nancy a rueful grin. "Very funny!" Then she shook her head. "To think I spent two years in Mrs. Dupont's class just so I could tell somebody that my aunt's pen is on my uncle's table."

"Never mind," said Nancy. "You can practice while we're here. I bet that by the time we leave, you'll be chattering away like a native."

"I'm sure I will. But listen, Nan, if I wink at you like this"—Bess slowly lowered her right eyelid—"you drop your pen on the table, okay? Then I'll tell you where it is, in perfect French."

Nancy laughed. "That'll impress them! I wish George could have come with us—we could have worked out a whole routine. Let's get in line so we can get out of here. Come on."

Up ahead at Passport Control the lines were dissolving into a confused mass of travelers. Everyone hoped to get to the baggage claim area a little ahead of the others. Pushed one way, then the other, Nancy felt her patience begin to give out. She had just sat on a plane for seven hours, and she was tired because although it was morning in Paris, on her time back in the United States it was still the middle of the night.

When someone pushed ahead of her in line, Nancy did lose her patience and tapped the guy on the back. "Listen," she began, "why don't you—"

The guy turned around, hands raised in a sign of surrender. His blue eyes twinkled, and he had a big grin on his face.

"Hey, take it easy, Nancy," he said. "It was only a joke!"

"Joe Hardy! What are you doing here?"

2

"Waiting to get my passport stamped, just like you. Hi, Bess," he added. "How have you been?"

"Super," Bess replied with a broad smile. "I can't wait to see Paris."

Nancy couldn't believe the coincidence of running into Joe Hardy at Charles de Gaulle Airport, in Paris. "It really is a small world, isn't it?" she asked. "Is Frank here, too?"

"Sure, right over there." Joe pointed toward the next line. Nancy spied the brown hair of Joe's tall, athletic brother. When Frank Hardy saw them, he smiled and waved, then beckoned Joe urgently.

"Uh-oh," Joe said, "I'd better get back. I don't want to lose my real place in line. We'll wait for you on the other side of the barrier, okay?"

"Great," Nancy replied.

Joe strode back to his brother, just in time to hand his passport to the security officer in the glass booth.

Nancy watched for a moment, then said to Bess, "I wonder if they're here on a case?"

Frank and Joe Hardy had earned excellent reputations as detectives. In their hometown of Bayport they were as famous as Nancy Drew was in River Heights. Nancy had worked with them on a number of cases, all with spectacular results.

"I guess we'll find out pretty soon," Bess answered Nancy as their line began to move.

When she got to the head of the line, Nancy reached into her carry-on bag, pulled out her passport, and handed it to the security officer, who took it from her and thumbed through the pages. Then he turned to the front of the passport and studied her photograph. "Ms. Drew?" he asked. "What is the purpose of your visit?"

Nancy crossed her fingers behind her back and answered. "Tourism."

"I see." He found a blank page and stamped it. "Welcome to France," he said, handing the passport back.

As Joe had promised, he and Frank were waiting for them on the other side of the row of glass booths.

"Nancy, Bess, it's great to see you!" Frank exclaimed.

"It's great to see you, too," Nancy replied with a quick warm smile. She and the Hardys had gotten to be good friends, and it was always a treat when their paths crossed. "I couldn't believe it when I saw Joe in line back there."

"What Nancy isn't telling you is that she almost bit his head off before she saw who he was," Bess added with a laugh.

Frank pointed down the corridor. "The baggage area is over there, but none of the bags will show up for another ten or fifteen minutes. What do you say we grab a cup of hot chocolate while we wait?"

"Sounds great," said Bess. Nancy nodded, and the two friends followed the Hardys to a little café with a view of the runways. Frank ordered four hot chocolates, then turned to Nancy.

"Well," he said, smiling, "what brings you to Paris? A new case?"

"Could be," Nancy mused. "Did you know that Johnny Crockett is in Paris to do a couple of shows on Sunday?"

"The rock superstar?" Joe shook his head. "No, I didn't—"

Frank interrupted his brother. "Wait a minute! There was something in the magazine I was looking at on the plane about him. Isn't Crockett one of the stars in the World Hunger Rock Tour?"

"That's right," Bess said. "They're here rehearsing for a few days before the concert on Sunday."

"Johnny pretty much put it together himself," Nancy added. "Of course, he is the main attraction, too."

"So where do you come in?" Frank asked as a waiter brought them their hot chocolates.

Nancy waited until the waiter had set the cups down before she went on. "Johnny's been hassled a lot since the tour started a couple of weeks ago."

"Like how?" Joe asked.

"Practical jokes, mostly," Nancy said. "Or dirty tricks, depending on your point of view. What it adds up to is sabotage." She sat back in her chair and crossed her arms.

"And that's where you come in?" asked Frank.

Nancy nodded. "Bess got a call last week—"

"From Alan Wales," Bess interrupted. "Do you know him? He plays lead guitar in Johnny's band," she explained.

"Bess met Alan back in River Heights when he was playing in tiny clubs around the area," Nancy continued.

She avoided telling any more of the story. Bess and Alan had been very close for a while. When Alan saw a chance at his big break in music, he told Bess a series of lies that put her and Nancy in terrible danger. Alan did rescue them in the end, but Bess couldn't look at him the same way after that. They stayed friends, even after Alan hit the big time, but the romance was over.

"Anyway," Nancy continued, "from what Alan says, this harassment is starting to get to Johnny. When Alan told him about me and my detective work, Johnny asked him to give me a call. We hope to wrap up the case by Sunday. Otherwise, we'll have to go on to Rome with the tour."

"But today's Friday," Joe said. "How much can you do in two to three days?"

"Don't ask, Joe," said Frank. "Did you forget who you're talking to? This is Nancy Drew. She'll have it solved by tomorrow."

"Thanks for the vote of confidence, but I did bring my Italian dictionary," Nancy said, laughing. "Just in case."

"We're here undercover," Bess added with a hint of pride. "Officially we're joining the tour's

6

publicity staff. No one's supposed to know we're detectives."

Nancy smiled to herself. Bess often claimed to have zero interest in unraveling mysteries, but the chance to go to Paris and possibly Rome and spend time backstage with some top rock stars had been too tempting. Besides, in a pinch, Nancy knew she could always count on Bess.

"I won't tell," Joe promised solemnly, with a mischievous glint in his eye.

Frank drained his cup and got to his feet. "Let's go see if our bags have come off the plane yet," he suggested, digging into his pockets for some change. "I bought francs before I got here," he explained. "This one's on me."

"Thanks, Frank," Nancy said.

"We have to look for Alan, too," Bess said to Nancy. "He said he would meet us after we got our luggage."

"You haven't told us yet what you're doing in Paris. Are you on a case, too?" Nancy asked.

"No such luck," he answered. "We came over for a conference on art theft and smuggling. It's being held at the Louvre museum."

"Art theft has become a very big business, you know," Joe added.

"When does the conference start?" Nancy asked, keeping her eyes open for the carousel with the luggage from their flight. "Maybe I can get to one of the sessions."

"It started Thursday—yesterday Paris time,"

Frank replied. "But we couldn't get here for the first day. I just hope we haven't missed too much."

"Hey, Nancy, look!" Bess said. "There's Alan. He hasn't changed a bit."

Nancy looked around. She recognized Alan at once, but Bess was wrong—he *had* changed. In the old days he had been just another rock 'n' roller, in jeans and a T-shirt. Now that he was a star, he was still in jeans and a T-shirt. But the T-shirt was hand-painted, the jeans were tailored from butter-soft Italian leather, and he was wearing a belt worked in gold and scarlet thread.

When Alan saw them, his face lit up. A moment later he was giving Bess a big hug, followed by two kisses, one on each cheek. "That's the way they do it here," he explained, holding her at arm's length. "Bess, you look great!"

Bess turned pink with pleasure. "You do, too," she said.

"Hi, Nancy," Alan said. He gave her a kiss on each cheek, too. "I really appreciate the way you dropped everything to come over to help. This tour's a big deal, you know, and Johnny—" Then he noticed Frank and Joe standing behind Nancy and fell silent.

"Oh, Alan," Bess said hurriedly. "Meet Frank and Joe Hardy. They're fantastic detectives who've worked with Nancy on some cases. We just ran into them a few minutes ago. Isn't that a fabulous coincidence?"

"Hi, Frank, Joe," Alan said, shaking their

hands. His expression was friendly, but he didn't say anything more about Johnny Crockett and the harassment.

"Excuse me," Joe said, looking over at the baggage carousel. "I think I see one of our suitcases coming."

"Maybe we should all go over," Nancy added.

Alan helped Nancy and Bess retrieve their suitcases and stack them on a cart. "I have a car outside," he said. "Follow me."

Alan started toward the door, but Nancy hung back to speak to the Hardys, who were wheeling their luggage in front of them. "Where are you staying?" Frank asked Nancy. "Maybe we can get together while we're all in Paris."

"I don't really know," Nancy confessed. "Alan, where are we staying?" she asked.

"Everyone's at the Hotel du Four," he said. "It's on the Right Bank, just off the river Seine and right across from the theater, so it's very handy."

Frank scribbled down the address of their hotel, then added, "We're at a place near the Louvre. All the conference people are staying there." He handed Nancy a card with the address and phone number.

Alan glanced over her shoulder at the card. "That's just a couple of blocks from us," he said. "You guys want a lift?"

"We were planning on finding a cab," Frank replied. "But if it's no trouble—"

"No trouble at all. Come on!" He led them out

into the glorious early morning April sunshine. All the bushes and trees were just budding, and they appeared to be painted with a light green watercolor wash. April in Paris—Nancy was enchanted.

A sleek black sedan was waiting on the other side of the crowded sidewalk. A short, dark-haired guy in a World Hunger Rock Tour T-shirt was leaning against the fender. When he saw them coming, he went around and opened the trunk.

"Jules," said Alan, "this is Bess and Nancy, who are joining the tour. And these are their friends Frank and Joe. I said we'd give them a ride into town."

"Sure, no problem," Jules said with a slight French accent. "You want to hand me your bag?" he asked Joe.

"Jules is one of the best roadies in the business," Alan explained. "The only reason we managed to talk him into dropping his other jobs and coming on the tour was that he knew we were coming to Paris. Jules is a nut for Paris, right?"

"I grew up near here," Jules said, taking Joe's duffel bag and putting it in the trunk. "Now my home is Los Angeles, but I like to come back to visit."

Nancy glanced around to see what she could do to help. The luggage cart with their bags on it was a couple of feet away. As she turned toward it, she noticed a hefty guy in black jeans and a leather jacket bending over it, a hand in the outside zipper pocket of her suitcase.

Frank must have seen the guy, too, because he called out, "Hey! What do you think you're doing?"

Instead of answering, the guy glanced at Frank, dropped the bag, and broke into a run.

"Stop him!" Nancy cried.

Joe Hardy, closest to the burly guy, took off running. "I'll get him!" he yelled. In a second Joe was dodging around pedestrians and baggage carts. Nancy watched as he narrowed the gap.

Before Joe could reach his quarry, though, the man had jumped on a powerful motorcycle waiting at the curb just ahead. The rider, in black from head to toe, kicked the bike to life and roared off, narrowly missing a bus.

Joe stared after the motorcycle a second, then headed back to where Nancy, Bess, and Frank stood, still stunned by what had just happened.

"He got away," Joe announced. "Sorry, Nancy," he said.

"That's all right." She began to go through the bag the man had been rifling.

"Are you missing anything?" Frank asked, concern in his voice. "Money, passport, traveler's checks?"

Nancy fumbled in the bag, then shook her head. "No," she replied. "Nothing's missing." Suddenly she caught sight of a piece of folded paper inside her bag she didn't recognize.

"Something's been added, though." She pulled the paper out. "This wasn't in there before."

She unfolded the paper and looked it over. Trying to keep the nervousness from her voice, Nancy read the message out loud.

"'Snoopers and spies get what they deserve. This is your only warning, Nancy Drew. Go home while you still can.'"

Chapter

Two

Bᴇss ʟᴇᴛ ᴏᴜᴛ a gasp. Frank Hardy took the note from Nancy, read it through again, and let out a long whistle. "That guy wasn't a thief," he observed.

"No, I don't think he was," Nancy replied evenly. She looked off in the direction the motorcycle had vanished.

Joe pounded his fist in his palm. "I nearly caught him," he said angrily. "If only I'd spotted him a couple of seconds earlier—"

"Hey, listen," Alan said, "at least you followed him. I wasn't paying one bit of attention. He could have walked off with the car before I noticed."

Bess put her hand on Nancy's arm, concern in

13

her eyes. "Nancy, I don't get it," she said. "That note—whoever wrote it had to know who we were and when we were coming."

"And why," said Nancy, finishing her sentence for her. "I know."

"I thought we had a good cover here." Bess looked confused and a little worried.

"We do, or did," Nancy said, "but it looks as if it's been blown. Alan, who knew why we were coming?" Frank and Joe were standing off to one side, and Nancy kept her voice low.

"Nobody, really," the guitarist replied. "Me and Johnny, that's about it."

Nancy glanced sideways at Jules, who was stacking the last of the luggage in the trunk. "Anybody else?" she asked softly. "What about Jules, for instance?"

Alan's cheeks turned pink. "Well, maybe. He might have heard us talking. Anybody might have overheard, I guess. Maybe we weren't as careful as we could have been."

"It looks that way," Nancy said.

"Hey, I'm sorry," Alan said. "I'm not used to this kind of work."

Nancy gave him a quick smile. "It's all right, Alan," she said. "When we talked the other day, I should have warned you to keep our visit quiet. We're going to have to be especially careful from now on."

"But if the person or persons we're after already know who we are—" Bess began.

"*Somebody* knows who we are," Nancy said.

"Somebody who has something to hide and doesn't want us to find out what, but that doesn't mean *everybody* will know who we are."

Alan frowned. "If everybody in the company does find out why you're here, it will be in the newspapers, sooner or later. I don't think Johnny would like that. It wouldn't be good for the tour."

Joe and Frank were still standing a few feet away, politely pretending not to hear the conversation. Nancy turned to them. "There's nothing we can do right now, and no way to guess how many people really do know. So let's get going. Ready?" she asked the brothers.

"You bet," Frank said. "I can't wait to see Paris," he added, changing the subject.

Jules slammed the trunk lid. "All set," he called. Alan opened the front door for Bess, then climbed in after her. Frank, Joe, and Nancy slid into the backseat.

As Jules accelerated onto a crowded expressway, he asked, "Do all of you know Paris? I can show you a few high points on the way if you like."

"Oh, I'd love that," Bess replied. She sat up a little straighter in the front seat, even though the only thing to see was the traffic around them right then.

The expressway started up a long hill, between tall retaining walls painted in bright pastel colors. "Watch," Jules said. "From the top, we get our first look at the Eiffel Tower. It will be straight ahead, to the left a little—there!"

"I see it!" Bess exclaimed. "It looks exactly the way I knew it would. Nancy, look—the Eiffel Tower!"

Far off in the distance Nancy could just make out the tall steel structure. She smiled at Bess's enthusiasm, but she had to admit that her heart was beating a little faster, too. No matter how many times she went to Paris, it always made her feel special, as if she were beginning an adventure of mystery and romance.

Frank sensed her excitement and shared her feelings. "Boy, am I glad they're holding the conference in Paris," he said. "It's great to have an excuse to be here in the spring."

"I'd like to hear more about this conference," Nancy said, turning to him.

"Not much to tell," Frank answered. "The organizers want to pool information about smugglers from around the world, and then they'll try to come up with countermeasures."

"It's a pretty high-powered group," Joe added. "We had to have our dad pull a few strings to get us invited." Fenton Hardy, Frank and Joe's father, was a former high-ranking officer in the New York City Police Department and was now an internationally known private detective.

Nancy laughed. "I bet every art smuggler in the world is wishing he or she could listen in." As Nancy spoke, she glanced up. Jules was staring at her in the rearview mirror. After he met her eyes, he looked back at the highway.

"We're entering Paris now," he announced. "This freeway runs all around the edge of the city. We'll cut across, though, through the streets. You can see a freeway anywhere, but the streets of Paris . . ."

Jules made a series of turns, and within minutes they were on a narrow, curving street, lined on both sides with interesting boutiques. The sidewalks were crowded with shoppers, and at an outdoor café on the corner every table was filled.

As they drove by, Bess said, "Nan, did you see that woman having coffee and reading the newspaper at that café? Oh, I wish we could just get out and wander around and stop at a café," Bess said. She leaned over Alan to look out the side window.

"Don't worry, Bess," Alan replied, putting his arm around her. "I'm pretty socked in with rehearsals, but I'll find the time to take you around. I won't let you feel neglected."

On the other side of her Jules coughed. "I'll be happy to show you around whenever Alan is too busy," he said. "You should see Paris with someone who knows the city. There are so many interesting places that you might never find by yourself."

Alan opened his mouth to speak, but Jules pointed to the left and continued. "On the other side of that wall, at the top of the hill, is the most important cemetery in Paris. Many famous people are buried there."

17

"I didn't know that," Alan said. "Maybe I can find time for a visit."

"If we had more time, I'd show you one of my favorite spots near here," said Jules. He seemed to be talking more to Bess than to the others. "Imagine a canal that runs straight through the center of Paris. The barges sail along, and then *poof!* they vanish into a long tunnel. Just ahead, when we cross the place de la Bastille, we'll be driving right over the canal."

"Will we be able to see it?" asked Bess.

"No. It's still in the tunnel here, deep beneath the street. Thousands of people drive over it every day, but I doubt any of them think that a boat may be under their wheels."

As he spoke, the car swept into a huge open square. Lines of cars were heading into the square from side streets. They met in a dizzying circle around the tall, green bronze column in the center.

"This is where the Bastille once stood," Jules announced, finding a hole in the traffic to pull into and join the flow of moving cars. "The Bastille was a terrible prison that the people captured and tore down at the beginning of the French Revolution."

He leaned out of the window to shake his fist at a driver who was trying to cut him off. A moment later they had gone halfway around the circle, and Jules was edging out of the traffic again and down a narrow street. On each side stood gray stone buildings sprouting dozens of brick chimneys from their roofs.

"We're pretty close to the theater now," Alan said. He glanced at his watch. "You might have time to meet Johnny before we start rehearsing at noon. Unless you're too tired and want to go straight to the hotel," he said, turning to look at Nancy.

Nancy straightened up. "We're okay," she told Alan. "We can rest later. Is that okay with you, Bess?"

"Are you kidding?" Bess cried from the front seat. "I can't wait to meet Johnny Crockett. Why do they rehearse so early? I thought rock stars went to bed at dawn."

"We do usually, but there's so much to do on this tour that we've had to change our ways. Rehearsal at noon—that's how it goes," Alan explained.

Jules turned to Alan. "Why don't I leave you and the girls at the theater, drive the guys to their hotel, then drop off the girls' luggage?"

"Whatever's best for you," Frank said. "Nancy, we'll call you later, after we're settled in, and see about getting together."

"Good," Nancy said.

The car went around two sides of a paved square and braked to a halt in front of a building with towering white stone pillars across the front. A row of statues of gods, goddesses, and musicians rested along the top of the pillars.

As he opened the car door, Alan said, "Here we are, the Pont Neuf Theater. Impressive, huh? I never dreamed I'd end up playing rock music in a Greek temple!"

"See you later, guys!" Nancy shouted behind her as she got out of the car.

Nancy followed Bess and Alan around the side of the theater and down a narrow alley to the stage door. The door was propped open, and no one challenged them as they walked inside.

"Isn't there a security guard?" Nancy asked.

Alan glanced around, irritated. "There's supposed to be," he said angrily. "You need tight security on a tour like this. Just think how many fans would like to get backstage to meet Johnny and the other stars. It's too early for most fans yet, so we're safe."

"Hey!" A tall guy with a long red ponytail was hurrying down the corridor toward them. His black sleeveless T-shirt revealed tattoos on both biceps. "Sorry, girls, you'll have to leave," he said, holding out his arm to usher them away. Then he caught sight of Alan. "Oh, hello, Wales. These girls with you?"

"Yup. This is Nancy and Bess. I told you about them. They're coming on board to do public relations. Bess, Nancy, meet Kevin Fuller. He's in charge of security. Hey, Kevin, how come there's no one at the door?"

"The stage manager borrowed my guy to help move some equipment," Kevin explained. "Can you believe it? People simply won't take our precautions seriously. Then, when something happens, who do they blame?"

Alan nodded and shrugged his shoulders. "You're right. It isn't always easy to do your job, is it?"

"You said it, mate," Kevin answered with a crooked grin.

"Is Johnny around?" Alan asked.

The security chief pointed over his shoulder. "Believe it or not, he got here early. I saw him in the greenroom a few minutes ago."

"Thanks. I want him to meet Nancy and Bess."

A wave of excitement washed over Nancy as she followed Alan down the hall. She could still remember the day she first heard a Johnny Crockett song on the radio. She'd made a special trip to buy the record that afternoon. Now she was going to meet him and even work for him. It was hard to believe. She glanced at Bess, who, from the expectant look on her face, seemed just as excited.

Alan pushed open a door and called out, "Johnny?"

"Yeah," a voice familiar to millions of fans replied. "Did they get here okay?"

From the doorway Nancy caught a glimpse of the superstar. Johnny Crockett looked just as he appeared on his record jackets. His blond hair, clipped short on the sides, stood up in spikes on the top. The color and style made his striking blue eyes stand out, and they emphasized his fine cheekbones. On his left earlobe he wore the Egyptian scarab beetle earring that had become his trademark.

Still, superstar or not, Johnny was obviously human. Nancy swallowed once and stepped forward. "Hi," she said, clearing her throat. "I'm Nancy Drew."

Johnny was slow to smile, but when he did, his grin was infectious. "Hello, Nancy," he said. "I'm glad to meet you. I want you to know how much I appreciate your dropping everything to help me out." He shifted his gaze to Bess. "That goes for both of you," he continued. "You must be Bess, right? Alan's talked a lot about you."

Bess, bright red, said, "Me? Really?" She gave Alan a warm glance.

"Have a seat," Johnny said, waving them toward a couch. "Do you want a soda or anything?"

"No, thanks," Bess and Nancy said together. They sat down, and Alan perched on the arm of the sofa next to Bess. Johnny pulled a chair up to face them.

"It's great you're here," he said, casually leaning forward. "But I'm starting to think I dragged you to Paris for nothing."

"What do you mean?" Alan began.

Johnny held up his hand, traffic-cop style, and Alan shut up.

"I think I let myself get all worked up over nothing," Johnny continued. "A couple of accidents, maybe a silly joke or two—what does that add up to? No one's out to get me. Why should anyone be? All of us on tour go back a long way together."

Nancy frowned. "When Alan called, he said you were pretty sure that these incidents weren't accidents or jokes. What changed your mind?"

"Nothing in particular," Johnny said with a shrug. "I don't see myself as the kind of guy who has enemies. I love everybody, and everybody loves me. Right, Alan?"

Alan glanced down at Nancy and Bess, then said, "Sure, Johnny, but still—"

The door opened and Jules walked in. He had a long white box under his arm.

"I took your friends to their hotel, then put your bags in your room," he told Bess and Nancy. "Let me know when you want to go to the hotel, and I'll take you across."

"What's that you've got?" Johnny asked.

Jules handed the box to him. "I found it on the desk near the door," he told Johnny. "It's addressed to you."

Johnny put the box on the table and opened it. "Hey, roses," he said. "I wonder who—"

He reached into the box. "What the—" he cried, pulling his arm back suddenly. Then he held out his arm and stared at it. The superstar's eyes became huge, and he started shaking his hand wildly.

"Do something, someone!" he shouted. "My hand! It's on fire!"

23

Chapter

Three

NANCY JUMPED UP and ran over to the stricken star. Alan and Bess were right on her heels.

"What is it, Johnny?" she demanded. "What's wrong?"

"My hand," Johnny gasped. "Something in that box made my whole hand feel as if it was on fire!"

Jules was staring at the box with a funny look on his face. Nancy joined him. The dark roses were lying on a bed of jagged-edged leaves. When she reached out for one, Jules grabbed her wrist.

"I wouldn't if I were you," he told her.

"Why not?" she asked.

"Those green leaves are *orties*," he explained. "In English I think you call them stinging nettles, and I'm pretty sure they're what made Johnny's hand feel hot and stinging. If you'll excuse me, I'll get some ice."

Johnny was gripping his hand and staring down at it. "My hand's starting to feel numb," he said to Alan. His face was pale, and there were drops of sweat on his forehead. "Do you think I need a doctor?"

Alan took one look at Johnny's swollen hand and was ready to agree when Nancy repeated what Jules had told her. Bess was dumbfounded. "Who would do something like that?" she asked as Jules returned with a tray of ice cubes and a towel.

"It's not a very funny joke," he agreed, wrapping the ice in the towel and holding it against Johnny's hand.

"It's starting to feel a little better now," Johnny said. "Thanks, Jules. I think I'd better sit down."

"Would you like me to bring you something cold to drink?" Jules asked. Johnny nodded. "Anyone else?"

"Okay, thanks," Bess and Nancy said.

"I'll help you." Alan and Jules left together.

Nancy went over to Johnny, who was leaning back on the couch with his eyes closed. "Do you still think you're just the target of a few silly jokes?" she asked.

Johnny opened his eyes, frowned, and reached up to touch his scarab earring. "I don't know," he said softly. "I don't know."

"Somebody sure does have a twisted sense of

humor," Bess remarked. "Not to mention a lot of money to throw away on roses."

"Good point, Bess," said Nancy. "Maybe we can trace the flowers." She picked up the box, taking care not to put her hand anywhere near the nettles, and looked it over. There weren't any markings—it was just a plain white florist's box.

She turned back to Johnny. "You were saying before that everybody in the troupe loves you. Just suppose that *somebody* doesn't. Do you have any idea who it could be?"

Johnny looked away. "Of course not," he said, touching his earring again. "I don't have any enemies. Even Roger—"

"Roger who?" Nancy said quickly.

"Roger Hart. You know—the lead singer from Volley. He's a big star, no question, but he keeps telling people that I'm trying to keep him down, that I'm afraid he'll end up a bigger star than me."

"What about that?" Bess asked gently. "Is it true?"

Johnny shot her a quick look. "Come on, Bess! I'm the one who asked him to join the tour. I didn't have to do that, you know. It's the biggest boost for his career since his last record made the charts. World exposure, great press, a TV special. Would I hand him all that if I were afraid of him?"

"Okay, so Roger is one possibility. Anyone else?" Nancy asked.

Johnny shook his head. "Not that I can think

of. Ruby takes little digs at me now and then, but I know it doesn't mean anything."

"You mean Ruby Bloom, the singer for Blue Roses?" asked Bess. "Is she on tour, too?"

"You bet. This is an all-star operation."

Nancy leaned forward. "Why would Ruby Bloom take digs at you?"

"Well"—Johnny hesitated for a moment—"she and I used to see a lot of each other. A whole lot. Then it came to an end, the way things do." He waved his hand in front of his face, as if shooing away an unpleasant memory. "It wasn't easy, for either of us, and of course she thought I was to blame. Maybe I was. But she got over it, just the same as I did, and we're good friends again. Besides, she and Roger are getting along very well now. Why should she resent me?"

"Ruby Bloom and Roger Hart?" Bess said. "Since when?"

Johnny held up his hands. "Hey, don't quote me! It hasn't hit the fan magazines yet, but since the tour started, they've been spending a lot of time together. That's all I'm saying on that subject."

"Both of them *have* had grudges against you at one time or another," Nancy pointed out.

"*Grudge* is a strong word," Johnny said. "We had some problems, sure, but we got over them. I keep telling you, no one is out to get me."

He reached out to put his hand on Nancy's shoulder. When his palm touched her, Johnny winced in pain.

Nancy looked at him through narrowed eyes. "I don't think French florists sell bouquets of stinging nettles," she said. "And I'm sure that little box of surprises didn't come here on its own. Maybe I should have a talk with your friend Roger. Do you know if he's around?"

"He was in his dressing room a while ago," he said. "Number four, down the hall."

"Thanks. Bess, are you coming?"

Bess blinked as if she had been daydreaming. "Oh, sure," she said, and headed for the door.

Nancy turned back to Johnny "We'll see you later, okay?"

"For sure." He looked deep into Nancy's eyes. "And listen, I'm sorry. Maybe I do need help after all. I'm glad you're here to give it to me. I want you to know that."

Nancy followed Bess out of the door, feeling slightly dizzy. Whatever that thing called star quality might be, Johnny Crockett had all he needed, and more. Being exposed to it at such close range was as disorienting as standing in front of the speakers at a rock concert.

One thing was already clear: she was going to have to watch herself around Johnny if she wanted to maintain any sense of perspective on this case.

The man in front of Frank and Joe finished registering and stepped away from the hotel desk. Frank took his place.

"I think you're holding a reservation for Frank and Joe Hardy," he said.

The clerk ran his finger down a printed list and said, "Oh, yes, monsieur. You are here for the conference." He handed Frank a printed form. "If you would not mind completing this."

While Frank filled out their names and home address, Joe leaned back against the desk and rested his elbow on the counter.

He was scanning the lobby as a set of elevator doors slid open. A red-haired girl stepped out and began to cross the lobby. She was wearing a delicate floral-print dress and a pale fur jacket with a big collar that framed her face. She glanced over and nodded at Joe's appreciative smile, but then abruptly she blushed and turned away. A few moments later, a few steps closer, she looked up at him again. This time, her glance was wary, almost frightened.

"Frank," Joe said urgently. "Look, isn't that—"

The girl's pace quickened. She was at the revolving door now. Joe started after her, dodging around two men with crew cuts and cigars. Just as he reached the door, however, a stout elderly man with dark glasses and a cane stepped in front of him and tripped. His cane became wedged in the revolving door, which came to a sudden stop.

Joe helped the elderly man to his feet and freed

his cane, then he hurried outside. A taxi was just pulling away from the curb. Through the rear window a pale face framed by a head of red hair gazed back at him.

Joe walked back inside and rejoined his brother. "That was Fiona Fox," he said. "I'm *sure* of it."

Frank glanced around at the crowded lobby. "Let's talk about it upstairs in our room," he said quietly.

After dropping his suitcase on a bed, Joe ran to the window to stare down at the street, as if the taxi might still be in sight. "I know it was Fiona," he murmured.

Frank lay down on the other bed and clasped his hands behind his head. "I'll have to take your word for it," he replied. "I didn't even get a glimpse of her."

"Not only that, I'd be willing to bet that the old man with the cane was really her father, Dr. Fox."

Frank laughed. "You should have seen your face when he jammed that cane into the revolving door!"

"I thought he was going to jam himself into it," Joe said with a grin. "If it *was* Dr. Fox, he sure was slick."

"Well, it's not hard to guess what Fiona and her father are doing in Paris," Frank said. "Take one high-level conference on international art smuggling—"

"Stir in one father-daughter team of top-flight international thieves and smugglers—" Joe continued.

"And you have the potential for very big trouble," Frank concluded. He suddenly sat up. "Hey, I wonder. . . . Where did I put that New York newspaper I was reading on the plane?"

Joe found it and tossed it to his brother. Frank rustled through the pages, then stopped. "I thought so," he said. "Listen to this, Joe."

Masterpiece Missing in Museum Burglary

Paris—Burglars broke into the Delatour Collection of Contemporary Art last night and stole two masterpieces by the late Pablo Picasso. How the thieves avoided setting off the museum's state-of-the-art alarm system has stumped the Sûreté, French Central Intelligence.

Each work is of an acrobat and was painted during the artist's Blue Period. The art theft squad of the Sûreté is taking special measures to prevent the thieves from spiriting these national treasures out of the country.

Frank studied the photographs of the two paintings, his face grim.

"I wonder," he mused. "Do you suppose our

31

friends the Foxes could have had something to do with this?"

"I don't know," Joe replied, "but I think we'd better find out. Unless I'm wrong, it looks like this conference may end up giving us some first-hand experience in art smuggling."

Chapter

Four

NANCY PAUSED just outside the greenroom and looked up and down the corridor. "I wonder which way number four is?" she said.

"Beats me," Bess replied. "Here's Alan, let's ask him."

The guitarist was carrying a big bottle of soda. "Jules is hunting up some glasses," he said. "Hey, where are you going?"

"To have a talk with Roger Hart," said Nancy. "Do you know where his dressing room is?"

"Sure, it's down there," Alan said, pointing along the corridor to their left. "You want me to come along and introduce you?"

"That'd be super," Nancy replied.

Alan set the bottle of soda on the floor and led them down the hall to a door with a big four on it.

"What is it?" a voice called out to answer Alan's knock.

Alan pushed the door open. "Rog," he said, "I want you to meet Bess and Nancy. They're going to help out with public relations."

Roger Hart was big, with the shoulders and upper arms of someone who pumped iron. His light blond hair and deep tan made him look as if he had stepped off the cover of a surfing magazine.

They had apparently interrupted him in the middle of a game of solitaire. Roger brushed the cards into a pile and shoved them over next to a coffee mug with an emblem Nancy recognized as belonging to the Summer Lightning Tour.

The rock star's white teeth flashed in a smile. "Public relations?" he said, raising an eyebrow. "The way things are going with this tour, you're going to have your work cut out for you. When did you blow into town?"

Nancy glanced at her watch. It was still set to U.S. time. "This morning," she said. "At least I think it was morning. A couple of hours ago, anyway."

Roger laughed. "Jet lag, huh? You'll probably get your head straight just about when it's time to hop a plane to another time zone. Nothing like life in the fast lane, right, Alan?"

"Right." Alan turned his attention to Nancy.

"Okay if I leave you girls with Roger?" he asked. "I've got to get back."

"Sure," Nancy replied. "We'll catch you later."

Roger leaned back in his chair. "Have a seat, you two," he said. "What can I do for you?"

Nancy hesitated, then spoke in her most professional manner. "We've heard rumors that the tour is having problems—a little tension between you and Johnny, practical jokes, accidents, stuff like that backstage. If we're going to be dealing with the press, we need to find out what's going on so we can field questions."

"You mean you can't cover up things unless you know what needs to be covered up," Roger said with a grin.

"I didn't say—" Nancy began.

"I know you didn't. Never mind, I'm just teasing. As far as I'm concerned, there's only one problem with this tour, and his name is Johnny Crockett. You find out what he's up to, and you'll know why all this stuff is going down."

"What do you mean?" Bess asked.

Roger pointed an index finger in Bess's direction. "Tell you what," he said. "I won't say a word about the way Johnny decides the order we appear in at the concerts. After all, the rock business is full of big egos. Why should he be any better than the rest of us? *And* I won't say a word about the way he put his own guy in to manage the tour. Somebody had to take it on, and Johnny's known Brent a long time."

35

"Brent?" Nancy asked.

"Yeah, Brent Travis. He's been Johnny's personal manager practically since the beginning. Where was I?"

Nancy took a deep breath. "You were in the middle of not saying a word about the way Johnny decides the order at the concerts or about the fact that he put his manager in charge of the tour," she answered.

Roger stared at her with arched eyebrows for a long moment before he burst out laughing. "I like you," he said. "What's the name again? Nancy? You're okay, Nancy. You've got nerve."

"Thanks," Nancy murmured.

"The thing I want you to think about," Roger continued, "is this. Paris is the fourth city on the tour, and we've been playing to packed houses all along. But the gate receipts are just covering costs. How come? What about all the money we're supposed to be raising to fight world hunger—where's it all going?"

It was Nancy's turn to be startled. "You think Johnny Crockett is ripping off the tour?" she demanded.

Roger held up his hands. "Whoa! I didn't say that. Maybe I've heard rumors, but I'm not going to be responsible for spreading them. All I said was that I'd like to know where the money is going. I'm not the only one, either. Sooner or later some reporter is going to ask the same question, and then we're all going to be in the soup."

Nancy was silent as she tried to figure out how the conversation had changed from practical jokes to an accusation of stealing from the tour. She was going to ask Roger if he had any evidence when the dressing room door banged open and a young woman with long, pure white hair rushed into the room. Her bleached jeans had rows of strategically placed rips down both legs, and she had on an open leather vest over a white T-shirt.

"Rog, did you hear the latest?" she demanded. Then she noticed Bess and Nancy. "Oh, sorry," she said. "I didn't know you had company."

"They're new to the tour," Roger replied. "Public relations. I was just filling them in on some of the dirt. Girls, this is Ruby Bloom."

"I know," Bess said, her eyes wide. "I'm a big fan of yours, M-Ms. Bloom," she stammered.

"Are you? That's nice," the star of Blue Roses said absently, turning back to Roger. "Listen to this: I just heard that someone sent his Mightiness a bouquet, made of some kind of flowers that sting. When he opened the box, he bent over to sniff them, and now his nose is swelled up as big as a tennis ball."

Roger gave a guffaw. "Great! Did anybody get a picture of him? I bet *Rock News* would pay a lot for it."

Nancy was amazed at how fast the news spread and how much of it had changed as it spread.

"They were stinging nettles," Bess volunteered. "They're supposed to be very common

37

here in France. And it was his hand that got it, not his nose," she added, correcting Ruby.

"Oh?" Ruby said, giving Bess a cold look. "Well, I'm going to hold on to my version. I like it better."

"Nettles?" Roger repeated. "You mean *orties?* That's too bad—I heard the effect wears off after only an hour or two. I was hoping it was something a little more long-lasting. Something like poison ivy." A sly grin passed over the star's face.

"You know all about *orties?"* Nancy asked.

Roger's grin grew wider. "Me? Sure. One summer in high school I came to France on a student-work program. We spent eight weeks clearing weeds out of flood-control ditches, and most of those weeds were nettles. It was murder at first, but we learned how to deal with them."

There was a knock, and Alan put his head around the edge of the door. He nodded to Ruby and Roger, then looked at Nancy. "Are you about done?" he asked. "I can take you over to the hotel if you like. You must be ready for a nap."

The word made Nancy yawn so hard that the hinge of her jaw gave an audible pop. The others laughed.

"Maybe I do need a nap," she admitted. "Can we talk again later?" she asked Roger. "I have a feeling there's a lot you could fill me in on."

"Anytime," he replied, flashing her another smile.

As she turned to leave, Nancy's foot bumped

the wastebasket. It went rolling across the floor, scattering its contents everywhere.

"Sorry," Nancy muttered, her cheeks burning. She bent down to pick up the trash. The first thing she touched was a piece of crumpled green tissue paper. It looked exactly like the paper that had lined the box of roses and *orties*. She glanced up and straight into Roger's face. His mouth was smiling, but the smile did not reach his eyes. They were hard and cold.

Sunlight slanted in through the cracks in the shutters and lit up Nancy's pillow. She turned over, squeezing her eyelids, then gave up, rolled onto her back, and looked up at the ceiling.

Finally she sat up. On the other bed Bess was smiling in her sleep. A wisp of hair had settled on her nose. It floated up each time she breathed out, then drifted back when she inhaled. The fourth time it happened, Beth sneezed loudly and opened her eyes.

"You were tickling me," she said crossly.

"Not guilty," Nancy replied with a laugh. She looked at her watch. She had reset it before napping, and now it showed one forty-five, Paris time.

"My stomach doesn't know whether it wants breakfast, lunch, or dinner," Nancy said, "but I do want something. How about you?"

Bess sat up, wide-eyed. "French pastry," she said. "Freshly baked bread and cheese! Hot chocolate! Anything. I'm dying of hunger."

"When you're finished dying," Nancy said, "get your shoes on, and we'll go look for a restaurant."

While Bess was getting ready, Nancy pushed open the tall French windows and stepped out onto the little balcony. The hotel was on the corner of a wide street that ran along the river Seine and another, much narrower street that led past the side of the theater down to the Seine. Turning to the right, Nancy could see the river sparkling in the afternoon sun. Reflections from the water danced on the dark walls of an ancient building on the far bank.

Nancy threw back her head and took in a deep breath. The air was fresh and exhilarating.

A movement in the street below caught her eye. The long black limo that had brought them from the airport pulled up at the curb, and Jules stepped out in a jean jacket and cap. He was crossing the sidewalk toward the entrance of the hotel when someone called out his name.

Jules turned. A big guy with short dark hair crossed the street and joined him. His black jeans, leather jacket, and sunglasses reminded Nancy of those on the guy who had slipped the note in her bag at the airport. Still, half the guys she had seen in Paris so far wore jeans, leather jackets, and sunglasses.

As Nancy watched, Jules and the hefty guy put their heads close together. The man was doing most of the talking. He was gesturing, holding on to Jules's arm, and talking loudly. It looked as if he was trying to convince Jules of something.

Jules walked away, but the man followed, talking and gesturing. Finally Jules turned back to him and nodded. The other guy appeared to be relieved as he reached into his jacket and slipped out a large manila envelope. He glanced to his left and right. Convinced that no one was watching, the man handed Jules the envelope.

The whole transaction took no more than a minute, but Nancy had the uneasy impression that she had just witnessed something no one was supposed to see.

Chapter

Five

Isn't it great to have our own private balcony?" Bess asked, stepping out to join Nancy. "And what a terrific view. Oh, look, that's Jules. Yoo-hoo!"

Jules quickly slipped the brown envelope into his jacket, then raised his head and waved. The dark-haired man hurried off, pretending not to know Jules. Nancy was more certain than ever that Jules and the other guy had been up to something highly suspicious. She wondered how she could find out what was in that envelope.

Cupping his hand around his mouth, Jules called up, "Come down and join me. We'll eat something."

"Super!" Bess called back. "Be right there!"

When they joined Jules on the sidewalk, he said, "Johnny sent me over to take care of you. He thought you'd want some lunch after you had rested. And afterward, maybe we'll go on a little excursion, to see something of Paris. We have to take advantage of such superb weather."

Nancy started to say that they were in Paris to work, not to see the sights, but she stopped herself. Jules didn't know the real reason that she and Bess were there, and if Johnny told them to take the afternoon off for sightseeing, it would seem strange to Jules if they didn't do it. The investigation would simply have to wait.

They walked a couple of blocks, past the theater and down a sidestreet, to a small café with a striped awning and two tiny white tables on the sidewalk in front.

Jules paused with his hand on the doorknob. "This is a little old-fashioned," he said. "I like it very much, but maybe you want something that is more with it? The OK Corral is near here, and we can get a hamburger there."

"Not a chance," Bess said firmly. "We can always have hamburgers back home, but you don't find places like this in River Heights."

"You have good taste," Jules said, and opened the door for them.

The place was half full. The waiter, in a formal black jacket with a long white apron tied around his waist, led them to a table near the back. Above them hung a huge painting of fields, trees, and distant mountains all done in muted colors.

As Jules was hanging his jacket and cap on a nearby hook, Nancy caught a glimpse of the brown envelope protruding from the inside pocket. If only she could get a look at it. . . .

Once they were all seated, the waiter said something, but he spoke much too quickly for Nancy to understand.

"Ah," said Jules, sensing her confusion. "Today the special is coq au vin—chicken stewed with vegetables."

"It sounds yummy," Bess said. "I'll have that."

"Me, too," Nancy agreed.

Jules spoke to the waiter, who nodded and went through a curtained doorway into the kitchen.

"I hope you like pâté," Jules said. "They make their own here, and it's very good. I said we'd all start with that."

As he spoke, the waiter returned with three plates of pâté, a basket of sliced French bread, a dish of tiny pickles, and a ceramic mustard jar. At the sight, Nancy's stomach growled.

The three were too busy eating to talk much during the meal. After Nancy had finished the last of the bread, she leaned back in her chair with a sigh.

Bess's eyes were gleaming. "Why don't we move here?" she suggested. "We could have meals like this every day."

"Now, for pastry," Jules announced. He motioned to the waiter.

Nancy groaned. "There's your reason," she told Bess. "A month or two of this and we would both look like blimps."

"A month or two?" replied Bess. She eyed the pastry cart loaded with cream-filled éclairs and napoleons, chocolate-iced petit fours, and tiny fruit tarts with butter-rich crusts. "It wouldn't take me more than a week or two! But wouldn't it be worth it?"

"I have an idea," Jules announced after they had devoured two slices of apple tart and one napoleon. "We must go to the Eiffel Tower."

"Right now?" Bess groaned. "I'm not sure I can move."

"A day like this, when the air is so clear, should not be wasted," Jules stressed. "From the top of the Eiffel Tower you can see all of Paris."

"It *would* be fun," said Bess.

"It sure would," Nancy said, glancing at her watch. "I should watch a rehearsal, though." And get started with my investigation, she added to herself.

"That's no problem," Jules replied. "We have plenty of time. Johnny is resting now and won't rehearse again until after five. *He* told me to take you to the Eiffel Tower. So you see?"

The only thing Nancy saw was that Jules was determined to take them to the Eiffel Tower. Why? Simply because it was such a nice day, and because Johnny had suggested it? Or did Jules have some other motivation?

"Okay," she agreed, curious. She drained the last of her coffee and pushed her chair back. "On to the Eiffel Tower!"

Frantically Frank looked around the cobweb-draped room. Joe was imprisoned behind one of the walls, but where? Frank had to find him and free him before his air supply ran out.

Tap, tap, tap!

The sound had come from the far end of the room, behind the huge, dark paintings.

Tap, tap, tap!

There it was again. It had to be Joe, pounding on the wall. But where was the entrance? How did it open? Time was running short.

"Joe!" Frank shouted. "Where are you?"

Tap, tap, tap . . .

"I'll get it," Joe said from somewhere close by.

Frank bolted upright and opened his eyes wide. Joe was walking across the hotel room to the door. Frank shook his head, trying to clear out the confusion. This was the first time he could remember jet lag giving him nightmares!

"What is it?" Joe called before opening the door.

This time Joe recognized the auburn-haired girl at once. And although his appearance had changed, the stout elderly man behind her in the hallway had to be her father. The last time he and Frank had seen them, they were walking out of a New York hotel carrying the priceless crown jewels of a small European country.

"May we come in?" Fiona Fox asked in the clipped, upper-class English accent Joe remembered so well.

"Uh, sure," Joe replied. He glanced over his shoulder. Frank was straightening the bedspread, which was rumpled from his nap. "The room is a mess, I'm afraid," he said, indicating the half-unpacked suitcases.

"That's all right," she said, following him into the room. "This isn't a social call. Good afternoon, Frank," she added. "You both remember my father, of course?"

There were only two chairs in the hotel room. The Hardys offered them to Fiona and Dr. Fox, then sat at the foot of one of the beds and waited.

Fiona looked down at her hands, clasped firmly in her lap. "I need help," she said finally. "We both do."

"What kind of help?" Frank replied.

She hesitated. "I should tell you that my father and I have changed professions."

"You mean you're not cat burglars anymore?" Joe asked gently.

Dr. Fox cleared his throat. "I have had problems with my health lately," he said. His voice trembled. "The constant stress, you know."

Frank nodded. Dr. Fox went on. "It seemed wise to find a less taxing occupation, one in which we could put our rather specialized knowledge to good use."

"We've established a firm of security consultants," said Fiona, "and we advise museums and private collectors how to protect their treasures against thieves. We're beginning to have quite a good reputation in the field."

Frank started laughing and was about to make a joke, but one look at the serious expression on Fiona's face told him it would probably be a bad idea. Instead, he asked soberly, "You were saying you need our help?"

Fiona looked at her father, who nodded, encouraging her to go on.

"It would cause terrible damage to our firm if people learned about our previous—occupation. Our clients only know that we are very experienced in security matters, but they don't know how we acquired our experience. If they did find out, we might lose our business."

"I get it," Joe announced. "Somebody's trying to blackmail you."

"Very astute, young man," Dr. Fox said. He pulled on his lower lip with his thumb and forefinger, then added, "The somebody in question is known as the Conductor. He specializes in transporting important and valuable works of art from one country to another without attracting notice from the authorities."

"A smuggler, in other words," said Frank.

"If you prefer. Naturally he knew of us, just as we knew of him. The top people in any profession all know one another, even if only by reputation."

"And now he's threatening to expose us unless we do what he wants," Fiona continued for her father.

"Which is?" demanded Joe.

Fiona hesitated. "He hasn't really told us yet—but we can guess. Did you know that several important paintings have been stolen from museums around Paris in the last few weeks?"

"The two Picassos?" Frank asked, remembering the article he'd read earlier.

"Yes, and others as well," Fiona confirmed. "The Conductor only moves the goods; he doesn't steal them. For that he needs people with very special skills."

"People like you and your father, you mean," Joe said.

"Quite right," Dr. Fox said.

"He wants us to pull off a job for him, I'm sure of it," Fiona added. A single tear ran down her cheek. "We don't know what to do or where to turn. We can't afford to risk exposure—it would ruin us. But we don't want to go back to—to what we were."

She paused to dab her eyes with a lace-edged handkerchief, then looked at Joe. "When I saw you in the lobby earlier, all I could think was that you were a danger to us. I ran away. But then I remembered how kind both of you can be. I'm hoping that you might help us. Tell me—am I wrong to hope?"

Joe reached over to pat her shoulder, but Frank

49

said coolly, "That depends, Fiona. Just what sort of help do you have in mind?"

"Well, no one knows who the Conductor really is. If we could find out his real identity, we could threaten to expose *him* unless he left us alone."

"Fight blackmail with blackmail, you mean?"

Fiona frowned. "You have a very nasty way of putting things, Frank Hardy."

"Sorry," Frank replied. "What if we identify your friend and turn him over to the police? He wouldn't be a danger to you then, would he? And the art world would be a little safer, too."

Dr. Fox cleared his throat. "I'm not very fond of the police," he said slowly. "But I don't care for being threatened, either. I'm willing to cooperate with your plan."

Fiona gave a quick nod. "If it's all right with my father, it's all right with me," she said.

Frank exchanged a look with Joe. "Okay," he said, "we'll try to help you. But we need a few more facts. How did the Conductor get in touch with you?"

"There was a message from him at the desk." Fiona looked at her watch. "Oh, goodness!" she exclaimed. "I have to be at the top level of the Eiffel Tower at four-thirty. And I have to have a specific guidebook in my hand. I don't have much time to buy the book and get over there."

"You think the Conductor is going to meet you there?" Frank asked.

"I'm sure of it, but if I don't get there in time . . ."

Frank sprang up. "You'll make it. Joe and I will get there ahead of you and stake out the rendezvous. Right, Joe?"

Joe was already slipping on his jacket. "Right," he said. "On to the Eiffel Tower."

Chapter

Six

W E'RE IN LUCK," Jules said. He pulled in behind a double-decker tour bus with a clear plastic roof and stopped the car.

"This doesn't look bad at all," he went on, scanning the crowds. "Sometimes the lines are so long you have to wait an hour just to get on the elevator."

Nancy leaned out the window and craned her neck to look upward. She caught her breath. Although she had visited the Eiffel Tower before, it always amazed her. From a distance it looked lacy and insubstantial, like a toy, but up close Nancy noticed again how *big* it was. There was probably enough room for half a dozen tennis courts in the space between its four legs. And since the tower had no solid walls enclosing it, it appeared taller than many skyscrapers.

"You'd better buy your tickets and get in line," Jules added.

Bess looked at him in surprise. "Aren't you coming?" she asked.

He shrugged. "I'd like to, but I have to stay with the car. There's nowhere around here to park. Don't worry, though. I have something to read while I wait."

He pulled a book from the map pocket in the door and showed it to them. From the title, Nancy decided the book was a mystery. A postcard that was marking his place fell out, and Nancy watched as he carefully found page twenty and put the card back.

"Well, all right," Bess said with a disappointed sigh.

Nancy gave her a curious glance. Was Bess working on a crush? If so, it would be interesting to see how Alan reacted. He and Bess had agreed to be "just good friends," but he still seemed a little possessive of her. Or maybe rock stars just assumed that every female they met was in love with them!

The clock on the dashboard read 4:05. "We'd better get a move on," Nancy said. "I want to be back at the theater in time to watch Johnny rehearse.

"No problem," Jules said, waving his hand in the air. "They won't go on before seven. In rock, everything happens two time zones farther west." He saw the puzzlement on Bess's face and added, "In other words, two hours late."

"Well, *I* don't want to be late," Bess replied, fumbling for the door handle. "You don't get to see a superstar rehearse every day. Come on, Nancy."

Bess climbed out of the car, getting her first real look at the tower. She stood with her head back, her mouth open, and her arms dangling at her side.

"What's wrong?" Nancy asked.

Bess continued to stare up at the top of the Eiffel Tower. "It's—it's awfully tall, isn't it?" she said.

"Uh-huh," Nancy replied cheerfully. "That's the whole point. The view from the top is fantastic."

"Really? How's the view from halfway up?"

Nancy burst out laughing. "Don't be afraid, Bess," she said. "You're going to love it!" When Bess still hung back, she added, "Of course, I *could* tell everyone back in River Heights that you refused to go up in the Eiffel Tower."

Bess looked at her, aghast. "You wouldn't!"

"Don't try me. Come on!"

Nancy led Bess to the ticket booth, then to the line for the elevator. She decided the family ahead of them was talking in Swedish or Norwegian. Just behind them, a Japanese father was speaking to his three children in reassuring tones. They kept looking upward with their eyes wide and their fingers in their mouths.

"It's only a thousand feet high," Nancy told Bess.

"That's an awful lot of feet," Bess replied. "Do we get parachutes?" At Nancy's grimace, Bess added, "I guess it'll be okay. At least if we go, we'll go together."

"Friends to the end," Nancy said with a laugh. "Oh, good, here comes the elevator."

An attendant opened a gate and directed the people near the front of the line up a flight of iron stairs to an upper level. Nancy and Bess were among the last he let through.

They pressed into the upper compartment of the elevator cab. It was the size of a small room, with windows on three sides. The door slid shut, and they were on their way. Within seconds the elevator was above the treetops, and the two friends were looking down on the roof of the nearby buildings.

"I don't like this—not at all," Bess whispered. "There's nothing around us!"

Nancy knew what she meant. The steel girders were just outside the windows, but beyond them was nothing but air—and a sensational view of Paris.

"Oh, look, there's an old-fashioned merry-go-round," Nancy said, pointing toward a little patch of grass between the boulevard and the river. She hoped to distract Bess, but her ploy didn't work.

"I can't look," Bess whispered. She turned away from the window. Her face was pale.

Nancy tried again. "Why don't we try to spot landmarks?" she asked. "I can see Notre Dame Cathedral, and there's the Arc de Triomphe over there."

Bess glanced over her shoulder, then shut her eyes and swallowed. "Just let me know when we get to the top," she said faintly.

Less than a minute later the elevator stopped and the door slid open for them to get out. They still had one more elevator to take to the very top. The passengers surged out, eager for the view from the railing. Nancy and Bess were caught in the middle of the flow.

The Seine was practically at their feet, curving around them like a letter *C*. Across the river a wide flight of steps led up through a garden to a long, low building that looked like a palace. Beyond it the rooftops of Paris stretched off into the distance.

"There goes a sightseeing boat," Bess managed to say, pointing to a long, glass-enclosed ferry cruising the river. "Do you think we could go on one?"

"Maybe," Nancy answered, her hair blowing in the breeze. "Don't forget that we're here on business. We can't spend all our time being tourists. As a matter of fact, I'm not sure we should have agreed to this little jaunt. The sooner we get back to the theater and go on with our investigation, the better."

"That's true," Bess agreed. She sounded a little

out-of-it. "There's rehearsal, too. I'm looking forward to that. But—Nancy, hold on to me."

Nancy turned to her. "What is it?" she said. "Are you feeling sick? Take a deep breath."

Bess shook her head. "No, *you* take a deep breath."

Nancy gave her a puzzled look. The only thing she could smell was that of something baking nearby.

"It's coming from over there," Bess added. She pointed toward a small snack bar. "And I know what it is, too—croissants with chocolate inside."

Nancy stared at her friend. "Bess," she protested, "we just finished lunch. You can't be hungry."

"I can't help it," Bess replied with a laugh. "High altitudes always give me a big appetite."

Nancy smiled ruefully. "Okay, okay. But make it fast. The crowd's lining up for the elevator to the top."

She followed Bess to the snack bar, then glanced over her shoulder. Out of the corner of her eye she saw someone walk by who looked just like Jules. The jean jacket and cap were the same as his, but his face was hidden before she could catch a glimpse of it.

Besides, Nancy told herself, it couldn't have been Jules. He was waiting for them down at the car.

* * *

Joe Hardy checked his watch. It was almost four-thirty—time for the Conductor's appointment with Fiona. She was standing just a few feet away, next to the railing, looking out at the view. In her left hand she clutched a red guidebook.

Joe glanced through a window into the room just behind him. Inside, on exhibit, was the office of the engineer of the tower, Gustave Eiffel, still furnished exactly as it had been when he was alive.

From the far corner of the platform Frank caught Joe's attention and raised his eyebrows. Joe shook his head, indicating he hadn't seen anything. Frank checked his watch again: 4:33. Was this going to turn out to be a wild-goose chase?

"Joe Hardy, for heaven's sake! Imagine running into you twice in one day!"

Joe drew back in surprise, then saw who had spoken to him. "Hi, Bess," he said in a low voice. "Listen, I'm on a stakeout. Would you mind—"

Bess took a step backward. "Oh, I'm sorry," she said. Then she turned and apologized to the man she had backed into.

"No damage done, honey," he replied, and went back to focusing the foot-long telephoto lens on his camera.

Joe joined Bess in a silent laugh. Then he checked on Fiona again, and the smile left his face. Frank was standing at her side, looking confused and angry. Both of them were searching the crowd with their eyes. In Fiona's right hand was a large brown envelope that hadn't been there the last time Joe had looked.

Joe rushed over to them. "What happened?" he demanded.

"We were hoping you could tell us," Frank replied, frowning. "A bunch of people got in my way. I couldn't see anything."

"Someone came up behind me and slipped this envelope under my arm," Fiona explained. "By the time I turned to look, he had vanished into the crowd."

Joe stared at them in dismay. "You mean neither of you even caught a glimpse of him?"

Frank shrugged. "A glimpse—sure. It was a guy in a denim jacket and a cap pulled over his eyes." He pounded his fist in his palm. "Some help that is."

"I looked away at just the wrong moment," Joe said. "I said hello to Bess and got distracted."

Frank gave him a questioning look, and Joe tipped his head toward Bess and Nancy. The two girls were a dozen feet away, by the railing, looking at the view.

"Maybe *they* saw something," Frank said. "Let's ask, at least. Fiona, you remember Nancy Drew and Bess Marvin, don't you?"

When Fiona looked over, her face hardened. "I certainly do," she said. "What are they doing here? You don't suppose they might have something to do with the Conductor, do you?"

— "Not a chance," Joe said with a laugh. "We ran into them at the airport this morning."

"They might be able to help us, though," Frank added. He beckoned to the two girls, who edged through the crowd and joined them.

"It *is* Fiona Fox, isn't it?" Nancy said. "I thought you looked familiar. The last time I saw you, you were disguised as a boy with short black hair."

Fiona shuddered. "Please! I have put all that behind me."

"Don't be too sure," said Frank. "Hadn't we better take a look at what's in that envelope?"

"I suppose so." Fiona slid her finger under the flap and opened it, then pulled out a thin sheaf of paper. The detectives watched as she quickly scanned the pages, then shoved them back inside the envelope. Her face was pale.

"What is it?" Joe demanded.

Fiona looked both ways, then said very softly, "This is a diagram of the new alarm system at the Berancourt Museum. Have you read about it in the papers?"

The others shook their heads.

"The old baron, whose father founded the museum, died recently," Fiona explained. "He left the museum a Picasso worth millions—"

She fell silent.

"And?" Joe prompted.

Fiona looked out over Paris. In a voice so low they had to lean in to hear her, she went on. "And now the Conductor expects us to steal it for him!"

Chapter

Seven

NANCY TURNED straight to Frank and Joe. "What was that about not being here on a case?" she asked.

Frank gave her a helpless look and shrugged. "We weren't—until now. Let's find somewhere to sit down, and I'll tell you all about it." He glanced over at Fiona. "If that's all right with you, that is," he added.

Fiona's pout told Nancy the girl wasn't too thrilled, but she politely managed to say, "Of course, if you think it's best."

A few minutes later they were all sitting at a secluded table in a café on the level below the top of the Eiffel Tower. While Fiona listened and chewed delicately on the tip of her fingernail,

Frank and Joe told Nancy and Bess about the mysterious smuggler known as the Conductor.

When they were done, Nancy was silent for a few moments, thinking. Then she said, "Fiona, could I have a look at the note that was with the plans of the museum?"

Fiona reached into the envelope. "If you like," she said, "but I don't think it will tell you anything."

As Nancy scanned the piece of paper, a satisfied smile appeared on her face. "Actually, this" —Nancy showed her one of the sentences in the note—"tells me quite a lot."

Fiona peered at the spot Nancy was pointing out. "What about it?" she said. "It merely means that he will pay us well if we do as he says."

"It's not what it means that I find interesting," Nancy replied. "It's the way it's said."

Fiona looked again and read aloud, "'Rest assured that your labors will be justly rewarded.' It is a bit old-fashioned, but don't you see—"

"Here, let me take a look," said Frank. He inspected the page, then lifted his head to Nancy and smiled. "Our guy is English, right?"

Joe leaned over the table and picked up the note. "I get it," he said. "*Labours* with a *u*. All right, Nan!" He sat back then and put his hand behind his head, elbows sticking out like wings. He gave her a self-satisfied smile. "Except that our guy could be French or German or anything else and have learned his English from an Englishman."

Nancy gave Joe a sharp glance. What was he upset about? Maybe he was mad at himself for not keeping a closer eye on Fiona earlier. She caught Bess's eye. Her friend's expression seemed to say "ignore him," so Nancy went on, keeping her voice calm.

"I didn't say I'd solved the case, Joe. But every piece of evidence counts, if we know how to interpret it." She handed the note back to Fiona, who replaced it in the envelope and stood up.

"I'm sorry to rush off," Fiona said, standing behind her chair, "but I must return to the hotel. My father will want to know what happened."

"We'll get in touch with you later," Frank said, rising to shake her hand. "Until then, keep a low profile. The Conductor probably has someone watching your movements," he whispered.

Fiona gave him a startled look, then nodded. With a wave to the others, she walked away quickly.

Frank watched her for a moment, then said, "Anyone else thinking what I'm thinking?" he asked. Because of their confused expressions, he explained. "Fiona is English, right? I wonder how she'd spell *labours.*"

"What are you trying to say?" Joe demanded. "Do you think she's trying to put something over on us?"

Joe's tone made Nancy wonder again. Why was he so on edge? A long time ago, before any of them knew that Fiona was a thief, Joe had had a thing for her. She thought he was over it, but maybe seeing her again had brought it all back.

"I don't know," Frank said in response to Joe's question. "But we do know that she and her father used to be professional thieves. We have only their word that they've changed their ways."

"But if she and her dad *are* still crooks," Bess asked, confused, "why would they confide in you the way they have?"

"One reason jumps out," Frank said. "Fiona wants us to witness that robbing the Berancourt Museum isn't her idea. That way, if the place *is* burgled, she can say she had nothing to do with it and lay the blame on the Conductor."

Joe gave a grunt. "Uh-uh. Too tricky. *Much* too tricky."

"I'm not so sure," Nancy said, nodding slowly. "That would explain why Fiona was willing to let me and Bess in on her problem. After all, it's not the kind of story you'd want a lot of people to know about. On the other hand—"

Nancy broke off in the middle of the sentence and thought some more. Was she really ready to pass on what were not more than vague suspicions?

"I recognize that look, Drew," Frank said, narrowing his eyes. "You're on to something. What is it?"

"Well . . ." Nancy said. "The guy in the denim jacket who gave Fiona the envelope—could it have been Jules?"

Frank and Joe faced her with puzzled expressions. She added, "The guy who drove us in from the airport."

"Jules!" exclaimed Bess. "Nancy, how could you say such a thing!"

But Frank was nodding. "I didn't see his face," he said, "but the height and build were right. Why?"

"Jules is wearing the same kind of jacket and cap as your guy," Nancy said.

"That doesn't prove a thing!" Bess interjected.

"Our visit to the Eiffel Tower was Jules's idea," Nancy pointed out, ignoring her friend's protest. "He drove us here, then said he had to stay with the car. But I thought I saw him a few minutes later on this level, making his way to the elevator to the top."

"You only *thought* you saw him," Bess said. "It could have been someone else."

"That's true," Nancy replied. "But just before Jules came to get us at our hotel this afternoon, I noticed him from our balcony. He was talking to a guy dressed in black, who handed him an envelope—a big manila envelope, exactly like the one Fiona was slipped. I think we have a right to be a little suspicious of Jules."

"What ever happened to the theory of being innocent until proven guilty?" Bess asked. "Or doesn't that apply now that we're in a foreign country?" she continued with a pout.

"Okay, Bess," Nancy said, standing up. "We'll

let Jules defend himself." She dropped some coins on the table, and all four of them trooped out of the restaurant.

Nancy and Bess led the others to the spot where Jules had parked. He was sitting in the driver's seat, reading his book. As they approached, he put the postcard back in his book to mark his place. Then he opened the door and got out.

"I see you ran into your friends again," he said. "Small world, isn't it?"

"I hope we weren't gone too long," Nancy said. "Did you have to stay with the car the whole time?" she asked casually.

"Sure, but don't worry about it. I had my book." He held it up, then tossed it through the open window onto the front seat.

"I can't believe you weren't tempted to go up for a look at the view," Frank said. "It's pretty spectacular."

"Yeah, I wouldn't have missed it for anything," Joe added.

Jules held out his hands, palms up, and gave a very French shrug. "It crossed my mind," he said. "But I've been up there a million times. Why spend the money to make it a million and one? Nancy, are you and Bess ready to go back to the theater? You don't want to miss anything."

"Sure," Nancy replied. "Do you mind if Joe and Frank come along? I want them to meet Johnny. They know a lot of newspaper people, and they can help me with my work."

She ignored the startled glances from the Hardys. There would be time to explain later.

Jules shrugged again. "It's all right with me, but I can't promise what Johnny will say." He climbed in and put the key in the ignition.

Nancy went around and opened the other front door. Jules's book was still on the seat. She picked it up and thumbed through it casually. "Is this any good?" she asked. "I'd like to try reading something in French but nothing too hard."

Jules reached over—a little too quickly, Nancy thought—and took the book from her. "I don't think this is for you," he replied. "This author's books are full of Parisian slang. Even some French people have trouble with him. I'll find something easier for you."

From the backseat Bess gave Nancy a triumphant glance. Nancy looked away. She wanted to believe Jules was innocent, but a small clue gave him away. According to Jules, he'd been sitting there reading for more than an hour, but his bookmark hadn't moved past page twenty—the exact spot it had been before they left.

Nancy let Jules and Bess go into the theater ahead of her while she lagged behind with the Hardys. "I suppose you're wondering why I brought you here," she said in a whisper. A smile turned up the corners of her mouth.

Frank put on a surprised expression. "To meet Johnny Crockett," he replied. "That's what you told our friend Jules, isn't it?"

She quickly told them about the bookmark in Jules's mystery novel. "Either he spent an hour reading one page," she concluded, "or he was busy doing something else during that time."

"Such as delivering a large manila envelope to Fiona Fox," Joe said.

"Which means the trail of the Conductor could very well lead back here, to the theater," Frank added. "You know, it makes sense. A big-name rock tour like this one crosses one border after another. That would be the perfect cover for a smuggler."

"Just what I was thinking," Nancy replied. "I don't know yet if the cases we're working on are connected, but they seem to lead to the same places. What do you say we join forces?"

Frank and Joe exchanged a quick glance. Joe nodded decisively. "Great," Frank said for both of them. "When do we start?"

Nancy tossed her hair back. "Right now," she said. "Let's go find Johnny."

This time there was a guard at the door who refused to let Joe and Frank pass until he checked with Kevin. A brief glimpse onstage told Nancy that the Blue Roses, Ruby Bloom's group, was rehearsing. Among those watching from the wings were Bess and Jules. Nancy decided that the two spent as much time gazing at each other as at the group onstage.

Nancy led Joe and Frank back to Johnny Crockett's dressing room and knocked.

"Who is it?" Johnny called out. When the rock star came to the door and saw Nancy standing there, he gave her a big grin. "Hey, Nancy! Where have you been all this time?"

"Bess and I just got back from a visit to the Eiffel Tower," she answered, stepping inside the dressing room. Frank and Joe followed her.

"On your first day? Pretty heavy stuff. I thought you were supposed to be taking a nap."

"I did," Nancy replied. "Then Jules came to take us to lunch and to the Eiffel Tower. I got the impression it was your idea."

Johnny shook his head. "Me?" he asked. "Nope, not guilty. Not unless he misunderstood something I said. Who are your friends?"

Nancy introduced Frank and Joe, who seemed a little awestruck to shake hands with Johnny Crockett. Nancy explained who they were. "They've agreed to give me some help with your case," she added.

Johnny went over to his dressing table and began idly sorting through a pile of cassettes. "Like I told you before, I'm not sure there's any case to help with."

"No?" Nancy said in a teasing tone. "How's your hand feeling?"

"It's still a little numb," he admitted. "Okay, so somebody played a nasty joke on me," he said. "It probably doesn't mean a thing."

Nancy took a deep breath. Convincing Johnny Crockett that he needed help wasn't easy. Could

69

it be he didn't even know how Roger Hart and Ruby Bloom felt about him? "Johnny—" she began.

Johnny held out his hand to her in an imploring gesture. "Nancy, listen," he said. "I've been thinking about these little problems, and I'm— Well, this tour—I put it together because I thought we could do a little something about a very big, very bad problem. Hunger. People are starving all over the world. If the papers start talking about who's out to get Johnny Crockett instead of about starving people, we'll lose the whole point. I don't want that to happen."

"I don't, either," Nancy replied. "I can keep my end quiet, but I think we have to catch whoever's behind the harassment. To do that, I need your support and cooperation. Do I have it, or don't I?"

He gazed into her eyes for a long time. At last he nodded. "Okay," he said. "I'll support you, but keep the whole thing quiet. We're trying to help hunger—not promote ourselves."

Disturbed by the intensity of Johnny's gaze, Nancy averted her eyes. She saw that Frank was staring at her curiously. She tightened her lips. He could think what he liked.

Johnny glanced at the clock on the dressing table. "I'm due onstage," he announced. "We can talk more later, okay? Nice to meet you guys."

He opened the dressing room door just as Ruby Bloom was raising her fist to pound on it.

"There you are, you skunk," she said loudly.

70

Some people passing in the hallway heard her and stopped to listen. "I want to talk to you."

"Sure, honey," Johnny said. "I've always got time for you. But talk, don't just call names."

"Who decided on the order of the acts on Sunday?" Ruby demanded.

"You know the answer to that, Ruby. I did. Why?"

Under her mane of pure white hair, the singer's face became crimson. "And you know the answer to that, too! Where do you get off, trying to make the Blue Roses into crowd warmers? We're a big group—we don't open for anyone!"

An irritated expression crossed Johnny's face. "All the groups on the tour are big, Ruby. Somebody has to go first. Besides, the fans love you, and they'll love getting to see you first thing. Think of it this way, it's a compliment to open."

"Tell me another, Johnny Crockett!" She waved a ring-bedecked fist in his face. "Do you think I don't know why you're doing this? You still have it in for me, and you want to sink my career. I may not be a big brain, but I can figure this one out. And I can figure out what to do about it, too. Don't think you're getting away with this, because you aren't!"

She whirled around and pushed her way through the little crowd of performers and stage-hands that had gathered in the hall.

"Okay, gang," Johnny said from the doorway. "Show's over, let's all get back to work."

Under the pressure of his glare, the onlookers

melted away. He stood there for another moment, then gave a snort of contempt. "Even backstage I can't take a drink from a water fountain without someone stopping to watch," he muttered to Nancy.

"Actually, I was planning on watching you rehearse," Nancy replied. "Would you rather I didn't?"

"That's different. That's performing. When I'm performing, it tears me up if people *don't* watch. Crazy, huh?" He paused to give her a meaningful look before adding, "And you I definitely want to be there."

Johnny's eyes lingered on Nancy's. Nancy forced herself to hold his gaze. Johnny spun around abruptly and sauntered down the hall toward the stage. Nancy followed but glanced back once to see Frank and Joe watching from the doorway of Johnny's dressing room. Once again Nancy found herself blushing, even though she had nothing to blush about. Or did she?

"Come on," she called back to them. "Let's watch the rehearsal."

Bess and Jules were standing in the wings, talking. When Nancy, Joe, and Frank came up, Bess said, "Hi. Was that somebody shouting before?"

"More or less," Joe answered.

Her curiosity satisfied, Bess turned back to Jules. "Tell me more about what it's like to live in Los Angeles," she said. "It must be really different from Paris."

Jules laughed. "It is. But excuse me, I'm on duty now."

Nancy glanced at the stage. The drummer, the two keyboard players, and Alan were already in place. Alan noticed Nancy and gave her a smile. Then he saw Bess and Jules next to her, and his smile faded.

Jules handed Johnny his guitar and helped him fasten the leather strap. Johnny waved to Alan, who cued the band with the neck of his guitar and ripped out an ear-bending power chord.

Johnny ran out to center stage, plugged in his cherry red Stratocaster, and did a flying split. As he landed, he launched into the famous intro run of his monster hit, "Set On You."

Nancy, Bess, Joe, and Frank watched spellbound. Seeing a video was one thing, but standing only twenty feet from a performer like Johnny Crockett was staggering.

Johnny jumped up, still playing a series of dazzling riffs, and leaned closer to the mike, getting ready to sing.

But at that moment an intensely bright electrical spark leapt across the four-inch gap between the mike stand and the guitar.

Johnny's hands instantly recoiled from the guitar, his mouth open wide. A deafening crackle of static blasted out into the auditorium. Johnny tried to move, but the electrical charge held him immobile.

Nancy rushed onstage, but before she could

reach Johnny, another charge connected with the star's guitar, harder this time.

The force sent Johnny flying backward. As Nancy watched in disbelief, the famous rock star crashed to the floor, twitched once, and then lay still as death.

Chapter

Eight

NANCY RAN to Johnny and was the first to kneel beside him. Johnny's eyes were closed shut, his face pale, but he was still breathing. She touched her fingertips to the side of his neck and felt a faint pulse.

Frank and Joe and dozens of stagehands and band members circled the pair.

"Give them some space," Frank said to hold back the others. "Is he coming to?" he asked, an anxious tone in his voice.

As if to answer his question, Johnny stirred and looked up at them. His eyes were blank.

"Johnny?" Nancy asked. "Can you understand me?"

He nodded, then winced with the pain of

moving his head. "Yeah," he said faintly. "I'm okay, just— Wow, what a jolt! Like lightning shooting out of the top of my head!"

Alan stepped out of the group surrounding them. "I think we should take you to the hospital," he told Johnny. "To make sure you're all right."

"And have it in all the papers tomorrow? No way!" Johnny pushed himself up on one elbow, then reached out to Joe and Frank, who helped him to his feet. "I'm okay, I said! A little dizzy, that's all."

Kevin Fuller, the security chief, pushed through the crowd and took Johnny's arm. "You need to sit down," he said. "Alan, give me a hand, won't you?"

As Alan and Kevin helped Johnny back to his dressing room, Joe spoke up. "I say we find the sound man and have a little talk with him about what went wrong with Johnny's equipment."

Frank nodded. "My thoughts exactly. That kind of malfunction doesn't happen on its own."

"Good idea," Nancy said. "I'll look for you in a few minutes." As the Hardys walked away, Nancy turned to Jules. He was talking quietly to Bess, who still appeared to be shocked. "That guitar Johnny was playing—where is it usually kept?" Nancy asked.

Jules frowned. "The Strat? That's one of his favorite axes. He keeps it in his dressing room, so he can play it if he wants."

"It was there all day today?"

"As far as I know," Jules replied. "I know it was there an hour ago. When we got back from the Eiffel Tower, I helped set up for rehearsal. I got the Strat from Johnny's dressing room, fined up the tuning, and put it on the stand just offstage, all ready for him."

Nancy furrowed her forehead. "Could anybody have fiddled with it while it was out there?"

"Change the wiring, you mean? Yes and no," said Jules. "I wasn't watching it the whole time. Somebody could have taken it from the stand."

"Could someone have done that in so short a time?" Bess asked, perplexed.

Jules paused and shook his head. "I doubt it. To change the circuits, you'd have to open up the guitar. You'd need tools and a place to lay it down and stuff like that. I can't see anyone doing that without somebody else noticing and wondering what was going on. Can you?"

Nancy gave a disappointed sigh. "No," she admitted. "I guess I can't."

Ruby Bloom rushed onstage and came over to them. "Where's Johnny?" she demanded breathlessly. "Somebody told me— Is he all right?"

"We think so," Jules replied. "It was plenty scary, though. It could have been a very close call."

Ruby's face was almost as pale as the white hair that was her trademark. "What happened?" she demanded.

Nancy stepped forward. "Apparently, his guitar shorted out against the mike stand."

"Right," Jules added. "He took one hundred ten volts through his body. No, I forgot, we're in France. Make that two hundred twenty volts."

"How terrible! I never meant . . ." Her voice trailed off.

"You never meant what, Ruby?" Nancy asked softly.

Ruby started to answer, then nervously pulled on the ends of her hair. "I, uh, I said some nasty things to Johnny before," she finally explained. "I was really mad. But I never meant to lay anything on him. That can be very dangerous, you know. Sometimes the negative energy in your anger can call down other negative energies."

"I don't think your anger gave Johnny's guitar a short circuit," said Jules with a smile.

"Don't scoff," Ruby replied. "Strange things happen every day. Much stranger than that. Listen, I have to go. I need to calm down."

As she walked away, Bess asked Nancy, "What was that about negative energies?"

"You got me," Nancy said, staring after the rock star.

"Here, take a look at that." Fred, the sound man, pointed his flashlight at the tangle of wires coming out of the back of the mixing board. Joe and Frank bent down for a closer look.

"Which one?" Frank asked. "The one with the orange tape around it?"

"That's it," the sound man replied. The Hardys had been watching him trace Johnny's mike and guitar cords for several minutes now.

"It looks pretty normal to me," Joe said.

"Yes and no," Fred said. "There's a crimp in it that I don't much like. Maybe it got pinched under the corner of a speaker enclosure. That could have damaged the insulation, grounded it out."

"Enough to let that strong a shock through?" asked Frank.

"I wouldn't think so. Fuzzy sound, even static, sure, but a hot short?" Fred shook his head. "Uh-uh. To get a short circuit, you have to have both a ground and a hot wire. That could be our ground, but the hot wire . . ." Fred fumbled around again in the web of wires. "Wait a minute."

Joe leaned closer. "What is it?"

"Stand back a little," Fred told him. "The cord to mike number three—that's Johnny's—is frayed right down to the bare wire. Somehow it got tangled with the power cable. Until I pulled the plug, right after the accident, that baby was carrying two hundred twenty volts!"

Joe sat back on his heels. "I don't get it," he said. "Wouldn't you have noticed a mike cord that was badly frayed during the sound check?"

"I check out every cable and plug in this show, every time we take down the equipment," Fred confirmed proudly. "The last time was in Frankfurt, last week. All the cords were in perfect shape then. I guess that one got damaged somehow when the guys were setting up here."

"That isn't your job, then," Frank said.

"Ordinarily it is," he replied. "But Roger Hart had some problems with the mike placement at Frankfurt. I tried to fix it for him, but I just couldn't get it the way he wanted. So finally he asked if he and his roadies could set up the mikes here. I didn't see why not, so I said sure."

"That's pretty unusual, isn't it?" asked Joe.

"Not really," Fred replied. "A lot of stars are very picky about their sound. I guess they have to be. Their reputations are on the line. They're the ones out front."

"If those wires *were* tampered with," Frank said, "it sounds as if Hart had the best opportunity to do it, right?"

"Tampered with?" the sound man said in alarm. "Wait a minute, you guys!" He stood up and pointed at the bundles of wires running to and from the sound board. "Look, this stage is a maze of cables. They get stepped on, tripped over, tugged, and twisted. And some of them get damaged. I have to replace a couple of hundred bucks' worth every week."

"Sure," Frank said, "but how many times do you get a hot short?"

Fred looked at him closely and thought for a moment. "Well . . . hardly ever," he finally agreed.

"Johnny could have gotten badly hurt," Joe said.

"You think I don't know that?" Fred asked. He was starting to sound rattled. "Look, I have to get back to work. The last thing I want is for this to happen again. I'm going to check every single wire personally." He turned back to the sound board to confirm his point.

"Thanks for your help," Frank said, straightening up. As he and Joe walked away, he added in an undertone, "I think it's time we had a talk with Roger Hart."

By the time they found Roger, Johnny Crockett had gotten to him first. Frank and Joe found Johnny and Roger at a standoff in the greenroom, surrounded by half a dozen listeners. Johnny's fists were clenched at his sides, and the veins of his neck stood out. Roger was trying to look relaxed, but Frank noticed a pulse pounding in his temple.

"You placed those mikes, Rog," Johnny growled. "You and nobody else. I thought it was funny when I heard about it, but it never crossed my mind that you wanted to electrocute me."

Roger's face turned dull red. "Come off it, Crockett," he said. "If I'd decided to electrocute you, you wouldn't be standing here making stupid accusations. Or maybe they're not so stupid. Maybe you have some other reasons for accusing me."

Frank felt someone push through the crowd to

stand next to him. He glanced over. It was Nancy. Bess was just behind her, her face pale. Frank raised his eyebrows questioningly, but Nancy just shook her head. Perhaps she didn't know what was going on, either.

"Sure," Roger continued. "This is just another part of your smoke screen, isn't it? You figure that as long as it looks like somebody's out to get you, the rest of us will keep busy trying to find out who's behind it. We won't have the time or the energy to ask any awkward questions about where the money's going."

Frank exchanged another look with Nancy, Bess, and Joe. What was Roger talking about? Why did he think Johnny would have created a short circuit in his own equipment?

"The money's going to fight world hunger," Johnny said tautly. "You know that as well as I do."

"I *don't* know it," Roger retorted, taking a step closer to him. "None of us do, and we never will unless you let us look at the books."

Johnny stepped back and shook his head. "No way. They're confidential."

"Why, Johnny? What are you hiding? We've been hearing rumors that you're building a new recording studio somewhere near Saint-Tropez," Roger went on. He stuck his jaw out with a look that challenged the superstar.

Then, for the benefit of the bystanders, he raised his voice. "They say your new studio is going to have the best equipment this side of

Muscle Shoals. That costs a whole bunch, buddy.
Where's the cash coming from? Your own pocket? Or the mouths of those hungry children you
talk so much about?"

"Take that back, you—!" Johnny swung a wild
right at Roger, who blocked it with his arm, then
drew back to throw a counterpunch. Frank
jumped forward. He grabbed Roger from behind,
while Joe and Jules pushed Johnny back from
Roger.

"That's enough," Frank said to Roger. "You
made your point. Cool down."

"Let me go," Roger panted. "It's none of your
business anyway. I'm going to teach that guy a
lesson!"

"In what?" Joe demanded. "How to make a
fool of yourself? I don't think you need to. He
seems to be as much of an expert as you are."

Roger tried to pull away, but Frank tightened
his grip just above the elbows. The rock star let
out a grunt. "Now," Frank said in his ear, "are
you going to be friends, or what?"

"Okay, okay! Just let me go!"

"Hold it," Johnny said from the other side of
the room. "I want to say something. Rog, you
said some pretty slimy things about me."

"That's just for starters," Roger muttered.

"I'm going to give you a chance to find out how
wrong you are," Johnny continued. "You come
with me right now, down to the business office,
and Brent will explain where every penny this
tour makes is going. I guarantee it."

Frank glanced at Roger's face, then let him go. Roger stepped away, massaging his arm. "We'll be able to look at the books?" he demanded.

Johnny scowled. "I don't even know if the books are here or back in the States. That's not my department. If they're here, you can look at them—until you're blue in the face."

"You've got a deal, Crockett. Let's go, now!" Roger swept out of the greenroom with Johnny trailing close behind. Ruby Bloom raced after them. Frank didn't waste any time. He nodded at Joe, and all four detectives followed on Roger's and Johnny's heels.

As they were passing the stage entrance, Johnny suddenly shouted, "Hey, Brent! Come here, we need you!"

A balding, bearded man in his forties was just coming through the doorway. He looked up, startled. "Me?" he said. "What for? Anything the matter?"

"Some of my fellow stars are a little worried," Johnny said. There was a faint sneer in his tone. "I told them you'd show them the books and explain where the profits from the tour are going."

"Now, you mean?" Brent said, blinking rapidly. "Tonight? I don't know, Johnny. Maybe in a day or two. It takes time to—"

"To cook the books?" Roger called. "We'd rather see them now, if you don't mind. Before anyone has had time to work them over," he added.

Brent stroked his beard a couple of times. "Okay," he said, "if that's what you want. But don't blame me if you don't understand them. Ordinarily, if I knew I was going to be explaining them to people without experience, I'd prepare an information sheet. But, of course, I haven't had the time."

The makeshift business office was in the basement, one flight down from the stage. As they followed Brent down the stairs, Frank smelled something in the air. Was it smoke? He glanced over at his brother, but Joe didn't seem to notice anything. Maybe it was his imagination, Frank decided.

As the business manager pulled a ring of keys from his pocket, Frank sniffed the air—now he was sure he smelled smoke.

Brent finally worked the lock and pushed the door in. Hot gray smoke filtered out of the room into the corridor.

The business office was on fire!

Chapter

Nine

Smoke rolled out of the open door. Frank and Joe took a step back to get out of Brent's way.

"Fire!" Ruby yelled, and turned, tripping over Nancy's leg. Screams filled the narrow corridor as the crowd tried to escape from the choking fumes.

"Let me through!" A security guard ran from the far end of the hall, carrying a fire extinguisher over his head.

"Everybody, *walk* to the stairs!" Frank shouted. "Don't run! There's no real danger. Take your time!"

The guard, bent over double to avoid the smoke, poked the tube of the fire extinguisher in the door of the room. His aim was perfect. With a loud hissing sound, the smoke changed from gray to white, and the flickering flames disappeared.

From the street came the distinctive sound of an approaching fire engine. Moments later four fire fighters in shiny metal helmets charged down the stairs. One of them threw open the access door at the end of the hall to let out the smoke. The others dashed into the office.

Nancy listened as inside the room windows were shattered, pane by pane.

"My computer!" Brent exclaimed, clutching his head in his hands. "My books!"

One of the fire fighters reappeared and spoke in rapid French to Jules.

Nancy walked over to Jules and asked, "What did he say?"

"It was a very small fire," Jules explained. "A wastebasket full of papers. There is no danger now. It is out."

Brent opened his mouth to speak, but a coughing fit interrupted him. Finally he said, "Can I get back into my office yet?"

Jules relayed the question to the fire fighter, then said, "In a few minutes. They are checking to see how the fire started. When they're done, and when the smoke has cleared, you may have your office back."

Another fire fighter came to the door with a desk lamp in his hand. He showed the lamp cord to the first fire fighter, who examined it, shook his head, and clicked his tongue disapprovingly.

Another burst of French, which Jules translated. "The cord was frayed from the wastebasket resting on it. This caused a short circuit, which started the fire. Defective electrical cords are very dangerous."

Nancy caught Frank's eye and whispered, "And this place seems to have more than its share of them, too."

He nodded grimly. "That makes three in one day," he said. "Either the tour is having a serious run of bad luck or someone doesn't have much imagination."

Bess overheard him and exclaimed, "You mean someone deliberately set it?"

"I can't prove it," Frank replied. "But the timing seems a little too perfect to be real."

"I'm going in there," Brent announced loudly. "I have to know about my records."

Roger stepped up next to him. "We all do," he said. "Remember? That's why we're down here."

The fire fighters filed out the door of the office, and Brent walked in, followed by the others. As Nancy took in the damage, she choked back a gasp. The room was a wreck. Papers were scattered all over the floor, sodden with water and foam. Near the window, broken glass glittered. The computer was still on the desk, but the monitor was lying on its side and the protective glass over the screen was shattered in starburst shapes.

Brent stood in the middle of the room, not moving or speaking. He appeared to be lost.

Finally he spoke. "And they call this a small fire? What would a big fire do?"

He bent over, then straightened up with a plastic case in his hand. He looked around the little crowd and fixed his eye on Roger Hart. "You wanted to see the financial records of the tour?" he said bitterly. "Here! Here's what's left of them!"

He lifted up the unlocked top of the case, then stared down into it. It was empty.

"Well?" Roger demanded.

"The disks," Brent said, still staring at the empty case. "All the disks are gone!" He let the case fall to the floor and frantically began to search the area around the desk.

"Are you sure they were there?" Johnny asked.

"Of course I am," Brent replied. "I was updating a file this afternoon when you came by to pick up that letter from the promoter in Stockholm. I shut down the computer and put the disks back in the storage case before we left. You remember, you forgot the letter and had to come back for it."

"Sure, that's right," Johnny said.

"If I'm not in the office, I always keep the door locked," Brent added.

Roger crossed his arms and said, "Are you telling me that all the records have vanished?"

"It looks that way," Brent said. His voice was thick with despair.

"Very cute, Johnny," Roger continued, looking

89

at his fellow star with narrowed eyes. "I should have known you were giving in a little too easily."

Johnny ran his hand through his spiked hair. The veins in his neck began to stand out again. "You want to spell that out for me?" he asked. "I'd hate to think you're saying what I think you're saying."

"All I'm saying is that it was easy for you to agree to show us something when you knew it couldn't be shown," Roger challenged.

Kevin stepped between the two musicians. He was half a head taller than either of them. "Come on, fellows," he said calmly, "let's break it up. We've had a long day, and we're all a bit over-wrought."

"That's an understatement," Nancy said to Frank under her breath. "I know I'm ready to call it a day. To tell you the truth, I'm beat."

"Good old jet lag," Frank said. "I think it's time to head back to the hotel and order up a room service supper."

"Sounds good to me," Joe said.

Bess covered a yawn. "Me, too."

"Tell you what," Frank said. "Why don't we all meet for breakfast tomorrow at that café behind the theater? We can compare notes and map out a strategy."

"Great," Nancy replied.

"I wonder if they have good croissants," Bess added.

Under Kevin's urging, the crowd had just about dispersed. Johnny and Roger, keeping their distance from each other, were the last to leave. Before Nancy left the room, she glanced back at Brent Travis. He was standing next to his desk, surveying the wreckage with an expression of utter fury on his face.

After saying good night to Bess and Nancy, the two Hardys made their way back to the hotel. Frank stopped at the front desk to ask if there were any messages for Frank or Joe Hardy.

"No, monsieur, no messages," the desk clerk said, handing Frank the room key.

As the boys started across the lobby, a middle-aged man with jowls, wire-rim glasses, and thinning black hair parted in the middle stepped up to them.

"Excuse me," he said in English with a heavy French accent. "I happened to overhear your names. Are you by any chance the sons of Mr. Fenton Hardy?"

At the name of their detective father, Joe and Frank stopped short. "Yes, sir," Frank said. "Do you know him?"

"Allow me." The man handed Frank an engraved card.

"'François Guillaume, Commissaire, Sûreté Nationale,'" Frank read. "Of course, sir. Dad noticed your name on the conference program. He asked us to find you and send his regards. He said yours was the one talk we had to hear, no matter what."

"He is kind as ever," the police official replied with a smile. "I noticed your names in the list of participants, too, and made a note to find you, too. You young men are also becoming quite well known in our field. That is good. One always needs new blood and new ideas."

Joe looked at Frank and raised one eyebrow. "Frank," he said, "do you think we should . . ."

Frank nodded slowly, then said, "Commissaire Guillaume, are you busy now?" The French policeman shook his head. "Could you spare us a few minutes? Something has come up since we got here, and we'd appreciate your advice."

"Of course," the Frenchman said. "The sitting room just beyond that arch should be empty at this time of evening." He signaled a waiter and ordered a bottle of mineral water, then led them to a small room. Once seated, he leaned back, folded his hands across his stomach, and said, "Now, what is your difficulty, my young friends?"

"Have you heard of the Conductor?" Joe blurted out.

Guillaume sat up so quickly that his glasses started to slide down his nose. "The Conductor?" he repeated as he pushed the glasses back up. "Yes, I know the name. I know it well. What of him?"

"We think he may be in Paris now," Frank said tentatively.

"Why do you think this?" the policeman demanded.

Frank hesitated. "I'm sorry, I can't really say at this point."

92

"Why, if I may ask?" The policeman's expression was a mixture of obvious interest and skepticism.

"It's much too vague to explain," Frank said, only adding to Guillaume's puzzlement. "But the idea that he is here doesn't seem to surprise you."

"Nothing more natural," said Guillaume. "As you must know, we have had several important works of art stolen lately. Smugglers like the Conductor are usually part of the scene at such a time."

"Do you know anything about him, sir?" asked Joe. "Is he dangerous?"

The commissaire leaned back again and made a steeple with his fingertips. "He is not known to be violent," he said. "But he is extremely clever, and he is also well liked and respected by his associates. Perhaps he is also much feared. In any case, no one who has ever worked with him has ever informed to the police. Not many crooks have a record like that."

Frank began to speak carefully. "So if somebody came to us and said that the Conductor was forcing them to work for him—"

"I should find that a small bit hard to believe," Guillaume replied, very curious now. "In those circles it is usually thought an honor to collaborate with the Conductor. Of course, if it were a question of someone with a special and needed skill—"

He paused and looked at Frank and Joe, inviting them to give more details. When they were silent, he sat straight up and said, "I told you the Conductor is not thought to be dangerous. But I may be wrong. A seasoned criminal who fears he is about to be exposed may take extreme measures to protect himself. Especially if he believes he is dealing with amateurs. I think you would be wise to tell me anything you know about the Conductor."

After a tense silence Frank said, "I'm sorry, sir, we don't really know anything. But if we discover proof—"

Guillaume shrugged. "May I have the card I gave you for a moment?" He scribbled something in the corner, then showed it to them. "This is the direct line to my office at the quai des Orfèvres. Anything you can tell me concerning the Conductor—anything at all—will be of the greatest interest."

He got to his feet and shook hands with them. "I expect to have a longer talk with you while you're in Paris," he said. Frank and Joe didn't miss the implied threat in his voice. "Now, if you'll excuse me?"

"Certainly, sir," Frank said. "And thank you."

When they were alone, Frank turned to Joe. "Do you think I should have told him the whole story?" he asked.

Joe frowned. "It's not ours to tell, is it? If Fiona and her dad are leveling with us, that is."

"That's a very big *if*, if you ask me. Come on,

let's get to bed," Frank said, leading the way to the elevator. "I'm about to fall out."

As Joe opened the door to their room, a piece of white paper fluttered to the floor. He picked it up and unfolded it. "'I must speak to you tonight,'" he read. "'F.'"

Frank yawned wide enough to make his jaw click. "Something must have happened," he said. "We'd better give her a call right away."

"No need." A voice spoke softly from behind them. "May I come in?"

Joe stepped aside. "We should have remembered we were working with a cat burglar," he said when they were all locked inside.

"A *former* cat burglar," Fiona retorted. "I haven't much time. This evening I received a phone call from someone named Bobby Peeler."

"That's a phony-sounding name if I ever heard one," Joe said, raising an eyebrow and looking at his brother.

Fiona shook her head impatiently. "No matter. He told me that he works closely with a mutual friend. If I need any special equipment or technical help with my new project, I should get in touch with him."

"Your new project?" Frank mused. "Meaning the theft of the Berancourt Picasso?"

"It can't mean anything else," Fiona replied. "He must be part of the Conductor's gang."

"Did he say how to get in touch with him?" asked Frank.

"Yes, and that's the oddest part. He said I could leave a message for him at the Pont Neuf Theater."

"The Pont Neuf?" Joe repeated with excitement in his voice.

Fiona brushed her hair back from her face and said, "That's right. I can't imagine why. Isn't there some rock group playing there now?"

"More than one rock group," Frank said thoughtfully. "The World Hunger rock concert is at the Pont Neuf on Sunday."

Fiona looked thoughtful also. "Is it?" she asked. "The Conductor said that he expected us to agree to his plan by this weekend. That's a curious coincidence, don't you think?"

Chapter

Ten

"WE WERE RIGHT, THEN," Nancy said, her eyes glistening with excitement. "The Conductor *is* connected with the tour somehow."

Nancy, Bess, and the Hardys were sitting at a table in the sunny café behind the theater. Frank had just filled them in on Fiona's visit the night before and her conversation with Bobby Peeler.

"It looks that way," Joe said. "I think we ought to have a talk with your friend Jules and find out what was in his manila envelope."

Bess made a face and half rose from her chair. The waiter, who was just arriving with a tray of croissants, jam, and hot chocolate, took an alarmed step backward.

"Sorry," Bess muttered. She waited until he

had finished serving and gone back inside. Then she focused her attention on her friends. "You leave Jules out of this," she said.

"Don't be silly," Joe began. "We can't leave people out of an investigation just because—"

Nancy put her hand on his arm. "Wait a minute, Joe. Maybe Bess has the right idea," she said. "As far as we know, the Conductor doesn't have any idea that we're on to him and his 'assistant.' The longer we keep what we know quiet, the more likely we'll be able to track him down."

She paused to take a sip of hot chocolate, then went on. "So far, the only people who know that we're detectives are Alan and Johnny. But if we start questioning people, we'll lose whatever cover we have. And if this Bobby Peeler is connected with the tour, he'll be warned and stay well hidden."

Frank and Joe nodded thoughtfully. "Hey, look," Bess burst out. "Isn't that Jules now?"

A pale blue motorbike came to a stop in front of their table. From under a hand-painted helmet Jules gave them a wide smile.

"How do you like my *mobilette?*" he asked, taking off his helmet. "I borrowed it from a friend. It's not chic and powerful like that big sedan Johnny rented, but you can see a lot more and have a lot more fun."

"It must make the traffic jams a lot easier to handle," Frank said.

"You can believe it," Jules replied. "And if it gets too bad in the street, I just ride on the sidewalk! Only kidding," he added, turning to Bess with a twinkle in his eye. "Hey, Bess, how would you like to take in a few sights and a lot of fresh air? I'd invite the rest of you, but I only have one extra helmet and seat."

Bess smiled at Nancy.

"Sure, go ahead," Nancy said. "We'll probably take a walk after breakfast," she said, looking at Frank and Joe. They nodded. "What if we meet you at the theater around noon?"

Bess's face brightened. "Okay, Jules, it's all set."

"Super!" Jules took the extra helmet off the package carrier and handed it to her. "Here, I'll adjust the chin strap."

Nancy watched him lean very close to Bess and stare into her eyes. No wonder Bess was falling for him. By the time Jules had adjusted the strap, Bess's face was flushed.

"All right," Jules said. "Climb on back, put your arms around my waist, and we're on our way."

He put his own helmet back on, gave Nancy, Joe, and Frank a thumbs-up sign, and took off around the corner.

Joe gave a laugh. "Boy, does she have it bad."

Nancy felt she had to come to her friend's defense. "It's only one-third Jules," she said.

"What's the rest?" Frank asked quizzically.

Nancy smiled. "The motorbike and Paris. Face it, people have been coming here and falling in love for hundreds of years. It's a tradition."

Suddenly, with no warning at all, a wave of longing swept over Nancy. Why wasn't Ned Nickerson sitting there with her in a Paris café? Frank and Joe were both nice guys, no question about that. At one time she had even felt a special warmth for Frank, but it wasn't the same. Ned was the boy she loved, and he was thousands of miles away, at Emerson College, instead of in Paris with her. It wasn't fair!

Nancy shook her head to make her mood vanish. She sat up straighter and nudged Frank with her elbow. "Look, across the street over by the stage door," she murmured. "Is that Johnny?"

Frank took a quick look. "I think you're right. But why is he acting so secretive?"

"And why is he dressed like that?" Joe added.

The rock superstar was wearing torn jeans, a black leather jacket, and a greasy-looking cap pulled down to cover his blond hair. His eyes were hidden behind cheap-looking sunglasses.

"If I didn't know who he was," Frank remarked, "I'd expect him to ask me for my spare change."

"Yeah," Joe said. "Or take it without asking."

Nancy tossed some money on the table and stood up. "I'm tailing him," she announced. "It looks to me as if he's up to something, and I'd like to know what."

"We're right behind you," Joe replied, and Frank added, "Let's go."

A block away Johnny started down the stairs to the métro, the Paris subway. The three detectives hung back a little, to avoid being spotted. By the time they reached the change booth and bought tickets, Johnny was out of sight.

"We'd better hurry, I hear a train coming," Joe said. "Which way?"

"He went down the passage to the left," Nancy said, taking the next flight of stairs two at a time. The train was in the station with the doors open, and—

Yes! Two cars ahead, a guy in a black leather jacket was just stepping on the train.

"Come on!" Nancy darted through the nearest door with Frank and Joe right behind her. The door crashed shut immediately. The other passengers raised their eyes to stare for a moment, then went back to their newspapers and books.

Less than a minute later the train glided into another station. They stood by the door, watching the platform up ahead, but Johnny didn't get off. Nor did he get off at the next station. Nancy spotted him as he casually sauntered out of the train and up the stairs at the third stop. She, Frank, and Joe slipped out of their car and paused before dashing up to the street.

They spotted Johnny crossing the only boulevard in a neighborhood of old buildings and narrow, winding streets.

"What does he want around here?" Joe was

studying the dusty windows and doors in need of paint.

Nancy read the shop signs as they went. "I can't imagine," she said. "This neighborhood seems to be nothing but small clothing manufacturers, and they're all shut down for the weekend."

"Look out!" Frank called.

Up ahead Johnny had stopped and was now glancing back the way he had come. Nancy and the Hardys ducked into a doorway and waited, hardly daring to breathe.

"Do you think he saw us?" Frank whispered.

"How could he miss?" Nancy replied. "We're the only people on the street." She peeped around the corner of the doorway. "Uh-oh," she said. "He's not there. He must have gone around the corner."

They tore down the street, then peeked cautiously around the edge of the corner building. Their caution was wasted. Johnny had vanished.

The three looked at one another in frustration and disbelief.

"This is impossible!" Nancy exclaimed. "He couldn't disappear that fast. Maybe one of the shops is open and he ducked inside."

Joe led the way as they took off, pausing only the barest fraction of a second at each of the tiny shops. There was no sign of life in any of them.

Several steps ahead of the others, Joe stopped abruptly and pointed. "Look!" he exclaimed.

"There's an alley, right through the middle of this block. He must have gone this way!"

Nancy and Frank were beside him in an instant. An archway led into a narrow, stone-floored passageway. The alley was covered with a glass roof that looked as if it hadn't been cleaned in a hundred years. The shadows cast by the iron framework made the dim passage seem sinister.

A faded sign on the side of the building caught Nancy's eye. It read *Passage du Caire*. Next to it, a stone sphinx's head glared down at the sidewalk. Nancy felt herself shiver a little.

"What are we waiting for?" she asked, trying to shake the cold chill that had raised gooseflesh on her arms. Her voice echoed twice in the passageway. "Let's take a look."

A few feet in, Frank pointed to a figure a block ahead. "That looks like Johnny."

"What now? Hang back or catch up?" Joe whispered.

"I don't like to stay too far back," Nancy replied. "We could really lose him. But this alleyway is so empty, he's bound to spot us if we get much closer."

"Uh-oh," Frank said. "Company's coming."

"What do you mean?" Nancy asked. Then she saw what Frank was talking about.

Halfway between them and Johnny, two guys appeared from a doorway. They took off in Johnny's direction, shoulder to shoulder, almost filling the passage with their bulky figures. Their footsteps echoed off the stone walls and glass roof like repeating rifle shots.

Johnny glanced back and saw them. His pace quickened. The two men broke into a jog, one swinging a length of chain and the other a short club.

"Let's go," Frank said. Like sprinters leaving the starting blocks, Joe and Frank broke loose. Nancy's start was slower, but she stayed close.

By the time the two thugs heard their pursuers, Joe was only three yards from them. The man with the club whirled and raised it ready to connect with Joe's head, but Joe flew into a leap that scored right on the guy's chin. Down he went, and the club clattered across the cobblestones. Its owner scrambled to his feet and began to back up the way he had come.

Frank caught up to the guy with the chain. He got off a left-right combination to the man's midsection before he had to dodge backward. The metal chain whistled in front of him, just missing his face. Then Frank was down. He had slipped on a rough cobblestone and was sprawled on his back, defenseless.

The thug drew back and raised the heavy chain again.

Chapter

Eleven

FRANK TENSED for the blow, ready to roll to one side, but Nancy ran in then and kicked his attacker hard on the left kneecap. The thug shouted with pain, dropped his chain, and limped away after his buddy.

Nancy and Joe helped Frank to his feet.

Frank swiveled his head in both directions. "Where did they go?" he demanded.

Joe pointed behind him.

"More important," Nancy said, "where's Johnny Crockett?"

They stared. The passage was empty. Knowing there wasn't a moment to waste, Nancy broke into a run with the Hardys trailing her. Twenty yards farther on the passage bent to the left and opened into a little sunlit square.

Squinting against the sudden brightness, Nancy saw no one, only a confusion of tiny streets that led off from the square. She searched desperately for any sign of Johnny.

Down one street she finally spotted him leaning into the open door of a black car. He was talking to someone in the front seat, and she had the impression that they were in the middle of an argument.

Nancy was pointing him out to Joe and Frank when an arm reached out and took Johnny by the coat sleeve, pulling him into the car. A moment later the car sped away.

Nancy stared at Joe and Frank. "Did you see that?" she demanded.

"I'm not sure what I saw," Frank replied. "That was Johnny all right—"

"Did someone force him into that car?" Nancy asked.

"I don't know, but I did memorize the license number!" Joe shouted, pointing to his head. "Come on, let's follow them."

"How?" Nancy asked hopelessly. There were only a few cars on the narrow streets, and no taxis.

"It's too late now, anyway," said Frank. "They're out of sight. What now?"

Joe frowned. "Call the cops?" he suggested.

"I don't think so," Nancy replied, shaking her head. "What would we tell them? That Johnny

Crockett just got into a car that drove away? They'd laugh at us."

"But he might have been kidnapped!" Joe exclaimed.

"It didn't really look like that to me," Frank pointed out. "Maybe those guys were friends of his clowning around."

"We're not going to find any answers to our questions standing around here," Nancy said. "Johnny may be back at the theater, where the people involved in this case are. I think that's where we should be, too. If Johnny doesn't turn up, then we contact Guillaume and the Sûreté."

After a few wrong turns Nancy, Frank, and Joe found themselves at the métro station and then a few minutes later at the theater.

Across the street Nancy spotted Alan coming out of the hotel where she and Bess and most of the members of the tour were staying. She called out to him.

"Hi, guys," Alan said after he'd crossed the street. "Is Bess around?" he asked with a smile.

The smile vanished when Nancy told him that Bess was off with Jules. "Oh," he said in a flat voice. "Well, maybe I'll catch her later. Thanks."

He started to walk away, but Frank asked, "You haven't seen Johnny, have you?"

"Not this morning," Alan replied. "But he's bound to be around. We rehearse at noon. See you later."

The three watched him cross the street. Then Nancy said, "We've got half an hour, then. Let's go over what we know, what we suspect, and what we need to find out."

"What should we do about Johnny in the meantime?" Joe wanted to know.

"I say we wait," Frank replied. "If he shows for the rehearsal, fine. If he doesn't, we'll look for him or contact the police. Okay?"

Joe looked unconvinced, but finally he agreed. "Okay."

They took a table in the sun at what was fast becoming their regular café and asked the waiter for three mineral waters.

"Okay," Frank said. "First question. Who were those guys this morning? Just a couple of hoods who happened to see Johnny go by and decided to jump him? Or were they waiting for him?"

"I can't swear to it," Joe said slowly, "but the bigger one looked like the guy who left the note in Nancy's bag at the airport yesterday."

"I'm positive it was the same guy, too," Nancy admitted. "But who were they? And why were they after Johnny?"

"And how did they know how to find him?" Joe added.

"He must have told somebody where he was going," Frank pointed out. "The more I think about it, the more I think that car was waiting for him off that square. It wasn't there by accident."

"So whoever sent the car sent the hoods, too," said Joe. "No, wait, I take that back. Maybe the hoods found out where Johnny was going on their own."

"I don't know," Nancy said. She fell silent while the waiter served their drinks and went back inside. "For that matter, I don't know if Johnny really is being harassed. He tried to convince us he isn't."

Frank took a sip of his water, staring off into the distance for a few moments. Finally he spoke. "Do you know what's bothering me? Those nettles weren't nice, but you could still see that they were meant as a practical joke. The frayed cables were a different matter. Johnny could have been killed. Is our joker stepping up his campaign?"

"Or is somebody using the harassment as a cover for a serious attack on Johnny?" Nancy said, finishing the thought. "That club and chain those guys were swinging meant business."

Joe shifted impatiently in his chair. "Well, we know a couple of things about one of those guys who was going to attack Johnny this morning," he said. "One: he knew when Nancy and Bess were arriving yesterday, and either he or whoever sent him must have known why. And two: he knew where Johnny was going this morning."

"How did Johnny find out about that passageway?" Nancy asked. "I bet it's not in any guidebook. Who was he going to meet? Or was he even planning to meet anyone?"

She was interrupted by a burst of high-pitched laughter from just around the corner.

"You *didn't!*" It was impossible to mistake the voice of Ruby Bloom.

The response was too low-pitched to make out the words, but the chuckle after them did come through.

"Shut in or shut out, it doesn't matter," Ruby said gaily. "Either way, it's outrageous!"

The low voice said something that sounded like a warning. A chair scraped against the sidewalk, and Nancy found herself peering at the face of Roger Hart. When he saw her and Frank and Joe, he said, "Hey there, how're you doing?"

Nancy kept her expression neutral and friendly. "Good," she replied. "Nice day, isn't it?"

"Great!" Roger answered quickly. "Well, I've got to run. See you later." A moment later he and Ruby were crossing the street arm in arm, going toward the theater.

"Did they sound like lovebirds to you?" Nancy asked, following them with her eyes. "Or co-conspirators?"

Frank drummed his fingers on the tabletop. "It's possible—very possible—that they're guilty," he said. "But let's not forget another possibility. What if Johnny really is embezzling money from the tour, the way Hart said? He might be staging the practical jokes himself—as a smoke screen."

"He agreed last night to let people look at the books," Nancy pointed out.

"Uh-huh—and when we got there, the office

was in flames and the records were missing," Frank replied. "Maybe the reason he was willing to let people see the financial records was that he knew they were *already* destroyed."

"*Were* they destroyed?" asked Joe. "That guy Brent seemed to think they'd been stolen. He wasn't too happy about it, either."

A breeze blew a strand of Nancy's reddish blond hair across her face. She tucked it behind her ear and said, "Do you suppose he was upset because the records were gone, or because somebody else might have them?"

While the Hardys were forming their answers, they watched Jules's motorbike pull up at the curb. Bess hopped off like a pro and unstrapped her helmet in one easy motion.

"I can't believe you're such slowpokes!" she exclaimed. "We've been all over Paris, and you're still sitting here!"

Nancy exchanged an amused look with Frank and Joe, but Bess was too excited to notice.

"I can't tell you how much fun we had," she said. "We went the whole length of the Champs-Elysées. We passed the president's palace, and we had to stop because his car was coming out of the driveway. There were about thirty police officers on motorcycles riding beside him, but I stood up and waved, and I swear he waved back. The president of France!"

"He must have thought you were a voter," Joe said.

Bess ignored him. "And then Jules took me to the Bois de Boulogne, which is a huge park, and we rented a rowboat. Oh, I wish you could have been there!"

Nancy found herself wishing the same thing. Not that she particularly wanted to go rowing, but she would have liked to spend the morning wandering freely around Paris. Still, this was not a vacation. She had to remember that she was here on a case. Once the case was solved, she might take a little time to enjoy the city, but until then she was on duty.

Wasn't Bess supposed to be working on the case, too? That was the original idea, but she was acting as if she had forgotten it. Nancy was aware of a little spurt of irritation at her friend.

"I'd better be going," Jules said, revving the motorbike. "I have to work this rehearsal."

"Thanks for this morning," Bess said. "I loved every single minute of it." She gave him a kiss on the nose, and Jules rewarded her with a beaming smile before taking off for the theater. Bess let out a dreamy sigh as she dropped into a chair next to Nancy.

"Alan was looking for you," Nancy said. She tried to hide her irritation, but Bess had known her too long. She sensed Nancy's mood.

"Are you all right, Nan?" she asked.

Nancy felt ashamed of herself when she saw the troubled look on her friend's face. "I'm fine, but I think Alan really wanted to see you."

"My face must be filthy! I'd better go wash and change. Will you be here awhile?" Bess asked.

"We're going over to the theater now," Nancy replied. "Johnny was—"

"Okay, I'll meet you there, then. 'Bye!" Bess shouted before Nancy could tell her what had happened to Johnny.

Frank was tracing patterns on the tabletop with his finger. "You know, Nan, we haven't even touched the other side of this case," he observed. "And I can't help feeling we're neglecting it."

Nancy was surprised. "The Conductor? But we decided that he has to be connected to the tour—doesn't he?"

"Maybe," Frank said.

"So, the more we find out about the people in the company, the closer we'll be to unmasking him."

"I know we agreed to cooperate, but let's not forget that we're cooperating on two cases, not just one. If Johnny turns up safe, I think Joe and I had better spend the afternoon at our conference. We may get a lead there."

Nancy nodded firmly. "Good idea. But you're right, Johnny is our main concern. Once we know he's safe, I can go to work on Fiona's message, the one about Bobby Peeler. I can try to track him and the Conductor down."

Frank gave a little laugh. "Track—Conductor —not bad, Nan." He furrowed his forehead and stared at the stage entrance to the theater. "How about this?" he continued. "A conductor's a band leader, right? And who's the most famous band leader on the tour? Johnny Crockett, that's who!"

"You really are stretching it, buddy," Joe observed. "If you ask—" He broke off in midsentence and sat straight up in his seat.

"That car!" he exclaimed, pointing. A black car was just pulling away from the side entrance to the theater. "That was it, that was the car Johnny got into. Did anyone see who got out of it?" Frank and Nancy shook their heads.

"We'd better get over to the theater," Frank said.

They paid for their drinks and hurried across the square to the theater. The guard at the stage door recognized them and waved them past. Starting down the hall toward the dressing rooms, they heard a band tuning up onstage.

Nancy stopped dead. "Listen!" she said.

A chord, and then the familiar run that led into "Set on You." No one else could play that intro like Johnny Crockett!

"Johnny's here!" Nancy exclaimed. "He must be onstage. Come on!"

She spun around and ran toward the stage. With no warning, strong hands reached out and grabbed her by the waist and pulled her into a darkened room along the hall.

"Hey!" Frank shouted as he and Joe were

tackled below the knees and rolled into the room. The door was slammed shut behind them, and a key was turned.

Nancy rushed to the door and twisted the knob, but the door wouldn't give. They were locked in.

Chapter
Twelve

THE MUSIC FROM the stage was building to a raucous crescendo, and Frank knew they'd never be heard if they yelled for help. He took charge, found the light switch, and clicked it on. Their prison was an ordinary dressing room. Hangers were scattered on the floor, and the empty, dusty shelves indicated that the room was not being used at the moment.

"Now what?" Joe asked.

"Wait." Nancy reached into her purse and produced a tiny lock pick, holding it up between her two fingers to show Joe. "We'll be out in a minute," she said.

"No good," said Joe. "It'll take too long. Those goons will be gone. Out of the way."

He grunted as he let loose with a karate kick that scored. The lock clicked and the door drifted open.

"The subtle approach," Joe said with a grin. "It works every time."

They rushed into the corridor and glanced in both directions. There was no sign of anyone except the head of security, Kevin Fuller, who was standing in the wings at the end of the hall.

"What's happening?" he asked them.

"Someone shoved us in a dressing room and locked the door," Nancy replied. "Did you see anyone run by here?"

"Nope. I stepped away for a minute and just got back." Kevin explained. "What's going on around here? This is turning into one of those days I wish I'd stayed home in California. A couple of hours ago somebody glued the door to Johnny's dressing room shut. It took three of us and a crowbar to get it open again."

"That must have been powerful glue," Nancy remarked.

"It was," Kevin agreed. "Nasty stuff, too. Get some on your fingers, and your hand will stay glued together until you find a solvent."

An image flashed into Nancy's mind. She was in Roger Hart's dressing room the day before. On his dressing table was a Summer Lightning Tour coffee mug. Its handle was broken, and next to it was a tube of super-strong glue.

She was going to have to have another inter-

117

view with Roger, and this time her questions were going to be much tougher.

"You'll have to excuse me," Kevin continued. He looked over his shoulder. "Johnny's about ready to come offstage for a break, and I have a couple of things to check with him. He got here just before he went on, so I didn't get to talk to him."

Kevin left. Frank, Joe, and Nancy looked at one another in silence. At last Frank said, "I have a couple of things *I'd* like to check with Johnny, too."

"Count me in," Joe said. "Coming, Nancy?"

"You guys can cover Johnny. I want to ask Roger Hart a few questions." She explained her suspicions about the glue. "I'll look for you when I'm done, okay?"

Joe watched her walk away, then turned to his brother. "How many guys do you figure it took to shut us up in that dressing room?" he asked.

"Interesting question," Frank replied. "One got Nan, and another one tackled the two of us."

"You think they were the same two guys who were after Johnny?"

Frank shrugged. "It's possible. But if so, it means they're probably attached to the tour in some way. Wouldn't they worry that Johnny'd know them?"

"He can't know every single techie and roadie," Joe said. "Come on, let's find out what happened to him this morning."

Joe and Frank stopped after about two steps. They saw Johnny just ahead, standing and facing Kevin. They appeared to be disagreeing about something.

"I like having our own truck," Johnny was saying as the Hardys inched closer. "Sure, if we send all the gear air freight, it will get there faster—*if* it gets there. But I don't want to see our instruments in Athens when we're in Rome."

Kevin started to disagree, but Johnny cut him off. "What kind of security risk?" he demanded. "Our guys check out the truck when they load it and when they unload it, and in the middle the customs guys usually take a look, too. You want to talk security risks? When was the last time you heard of anyone putting a bomb in a truck full of electric guitars?"

He turned away from Kevin, who rolled his eyes in exasperation and strode away. The discussion was obviously finished as far as Johnny was concerned. "You have a minute, Johnny?" Joe asked, moving up.

"Yeah. Hey, I need to talk to you guys, anyway," the superstar replied. He put one hand on Joe's shoulder and one on Frank's, and nudged them in the direction of his dressing room.

"I've changed my mind about these jokes," he said. He was speaking in a low voice filled with barely controlled anger. "Did you hear what happened this morning? Somebody glued my dressing room door shut. It had to be somebody

119

in the company, and that really ticks me off. When I think what I've done to put this tour together, only to get sniped at by my own side!"

"But you weren't here to see your door glued shut, were you? We know that wasn't the only thing that happened to you this morning," Joe said very quietly.

Johnny stopped and faced him. "What do you mean?"

"Does the Passage du Caire mean anything to you?"

Johnny's mouth became a straight, tight line. "You guys followed me! Was that you who—" Then he shook his head. "No, of course not. But who—"

"Would you mind telling us what you were doing there?" Frank asked mildly.

"That's none of your business!" Johnny snapped, then he stopped and considered. "On the other hand, maybe it is, in a way."

He glanced around to see if anyone else was nearby. "Keep this to yourselves, okay?" he said softly. "I was scouting locations for my next music video. We've got an absolutely dynamite concept, but we need to keep it secret. That's why I went to that place on my own, without telling anyone."

Joe glanced over at Frank and caught an expression of surprise and suspicion on his face. "Let me get this straight," said Frank. "You didn't tell *anyone* that you were going there?"

Johnny nodded. "Then why did we see someone pick you up in a car?" he asked.

"That was my manager, Brent," Johnny said easily. "I wanted him to see the place, too, to give me his reaction, but I couldn't find him. That's why I went on my own, but I left him a note asking him to meet me there if he could."

"And he did?"

"Sure. We went around to check out some other possible locations, then came back to the theater together. You can ask him if you like."

"I don't think that's necessary," Joe said. "This note for him—where did you leave it? Downstairs, in his office?"

"No, he keeps his office locked when he's not around. I left it in his box." He saw that Joe didn't understand and added, "The mailboxes, over near the stage entrance."

Joe glanced over his shoulder. Near the security guard's desk, against the wall, stood a wooden case with rows of cubbyholes. "Oh, right," he said. "Was the note in an envelope?"

Johnny frowned. "I folded it, that's all. If you can't trust the people you're working with, who can you trust?"

"Good question," Frank observed. "What happened at the Passage du Caire this morning?"

Johnny rubbed his head and said, "You probably know better than I do. I was just walking along, drinking in the vibes of this place. Then I looked back and saw those two hoods following

121

me. They looked like trouble, so I split in a hurry. They must have run into some opposition, though, because as I was leaving I heard fighting. Hey, was that you guys?"

Frank nodded. "And Nancy. I guess they must have been nervous about drawing attention, because they ran off after a minute or two. I noticed you did, too, by the way."

"Meaning what?" Johnny demanded.

"Nothing in particular," Frank replied. "But you didn't come back to see what had happened, did you? You just got into that car and drove off."

Johnny's shoulders slumped. Then he straightened up and said, "Listen, you guys, there I was, alone in a strange part of a strange town, nobody around. Except those two from the annual mugger's convention. Sure I made it out of there as fast as I could. Why not? I didn't know you were back there. If I had, I would have at least offered you a lift."

"I see your point," Frank said apologetically. "But what about those two guys? Do you have any idea who they were or what they wanted?"

"My wallet, I guess," Johnny replied evenly.

Frank remembered how Johnny was dressed and didn't think anyone would have been after his wallet.

"They didn't look like they were after an autograph," Johnny continued. "As for who they were, I don't have a clue."

Joe grinned and said, "We'll see if we can't turn some up. That's our business, after all."

Nancy finally found Roger in a basement room, playing Ping-Pong with someone she recognized as a roadie. A plan formed in her mind right then. She paused out of sight for a moment and fiddled with her shoe, then went in to watch.

Roger tried to win a long volley with a slam, but his paddle grazed the edge of the table. It flew out of his hand, spinning through the air end over end. He backed away from it and stepped squarely on the ball.

"That's it," he said, picking up the flattened ball and studying it gloomily. "When you're having one of those days, all you can do is try to get through it alive. Let's call it a draw, Josh."

As his partner left, Roger glanced over at Nancy. "It's a good thing my luck was bad before you walked in," he said. "Otherwise, I'd be tempted to think you're a jinx."

"Speaking of bad luck," Nancy said, "Johnny seems to be having more than his share."

"You think so? I think he's just starting to get what he deserves."

"Nearly getting electrocuted by his own guitar? That's pretty extreme, isn't it?"

Nancy scanned the rock star's eyes for some kind of reaction, but Roger only shook his head sharply. "I don't mean that," he said. "That was a freak accident. But the bouquet with a sting to it was kind of cute. Somebody decided to say it with flowers!"

"What about the fire last night? Do you think that was an accident, too?"

"I don't believe that was an accident for a minute," Roger blurted out. "That fire happened just when Johnny needed it to happen. I don't want to mess up your new romance, but—"

Nancy interrupted. "What new romance?"

Roger rolled his eyes. "Oh, come on, sweetheart. Get serious! We've seen those heavy looks you keep getting from the Big Enchilada. You think we don't know why he put you on the staff of the tour? And your friend, the one who knew Alan in the old days?"

Nancy started to point out that she and Johnny had first met only the day before, but she stopped herself. If people thought that she was Johnny's new girlfriend, there would be even less reason for them to question her public relations job. In a way, it made her cover perfect—hers and Bess's, too.

Then another thought struck her. What if Roger was right about Johnny? He did stare at her intensely, but she had simply assumed he did that with every girl he talked to. She was going to have to watch out. The last thing she needed in the middle of an investigation was romantic complications with a rock superstar.

"Look, Johnny and I are just friends," she began. "I'd hate for any gossip— Ouch!" As she took a step toward Roger, her ankle twisted under her. She clutched the edge of the Ping-Pong table to steady herself.

"Wouldn't you know it," she said, pretending to be angry. "That heel came loose again!" She slipped off her flat and held it up for him to see. "And I don't even know the French word for shoemaker!"

"Tough luck," Roger said with a shrug.

"I know what," Nancy mused, going on with her act. "Maybe I can fix it myself. You don't happen to have any really strong glue, do you?"

"Sure," Roger said. "There's a tube in my—" A wary look passed over his face. "Wait a minute, I forgot. I left it at the theater in London. Why don't you try a hardware store?"

Nancy laughed. "I don't know the word for that, either! Never mind, I'll use sign language. I'd better get it, though. I can't go limping around Paris. See you later."

On the way back upstairs Nancy went by the business office. The door was ajar, and she could see Brent Travis sorting through soggy papers.

"Hi," she said, knocking lightly and stepping inside. "Any luck finding those disks?"

"Disks?" Travis asked, confused. "Oh, you mean the ones I mentioned losing last night?"

His change in attitude intrigued Nancy. "All the financial records of the tour," she reminded him.

"Did I say that?" he replied, stroking his

beard. "I must have been overexcited. No, no, all the records of the tour are safe in my office in L.A. What I had here were just working copies."

"You seemed awfully upset about them last night," Nancy remarked.

"How would you feel if you came back from dinner and found your office in flames?" he asked.

Nancy studied his face. Her questions were beginning to arouse his suspicions, but the missing disks continued to bother her. "Then you don't really care if the disks were lost in the fire?"

He shrugged one shoulder. "Not really. It's an inconvenience, that's all. I called L.A. last night and asked them to send me another set."

Nancy probed. "What if somebody stole them? Would that disturb you?"

Brent shrugged. "Those are confidential records. I don't like the idea of some outsider getting hold of them, but we don't have anything to hide. Remember, Johnny was ready to show them to everybody last night. Listen, I hate to be rude, but I have a lot of work to do here. Would you mind?"

"Oh, sure," Nancy said. "Sorry to bother you."

She climbed the stairs to the stage level and found Johnny, Frank, and Joe talking in the hallway a few feet away.

Out of the corner of her eye, Nancy noticed a sudden movement. She quickly glanced up the spiral stairs to the next floor. At that moment, two red balloons that seemed to be filled with liquid came hurtling down the stairwell. They were heading straight for Johnny, Frank, and Joe.

"Look out!" she yelled, but her shout was cut short as the balloons struck the floor, broke open, and the liquids mixed. The hallway reeked of the odor of ammonia and laundry bleach, but the boys had jumped out of the direct line of fire.

Nancy felt a rasping cough form in her throat. A thin layer of oily greenish gas was beginning to flow slowly across the floor.

"Everybody back!" she cried. "Clear the area! That's chlorine gas. And it's poisonous!"

Chapter

Thirteen

Come on, Frank," Joe shouted. "Let's get some air in here!"

While Nancy urged everyone out the stage entrance to the street, the two brothers ran to the huge sliding doors at the back, next to the loading dock, and forced them open. A fresh breeze swept through the backstage area.

"Here, what's all this about?" A security guard came running, with Kevin close behind. "Who authorized you to open those?"

Joe began to explain. The gas was starting to dissipate, but it was still strong enough for the security chief to smell. He ordered his guards to clear the area.

"You fellows had better be on your way, too,"

he added, turning back to Joe and Frank. "We don't want anyone getting sick, do we?"

Joe caught Frank's eye and gave a tiny nod. The two of them started in the direction of the stage entrance, but as soon as they were out of Kevin's hearing, Joe muttered, "That little surprise was thrown from upstairs. Let's take a look."

As they reached the spiral staircase, Joe glanced back. Kevin had his back to them, talking to his guards.

"Now," Joe said. They sprinted up the stairs.

They were in a long, dimly lit hallway, lined with numbered doors. "More dressing rooms," Frank guessed. He tried the nearest door. It was locked.

"It looks as if someone left in a hurry," Joe remarked, pointing to a half-open door at the end of the hallway.

They walked in its direction. Under the number eleven painted on the door was a small thumbtacked card that read "Ruby Bloom."

Frank pushed the door open, looked inside, and whistled softly. On the dressing table a bottle of liquid makeup base had overturned, spilling a river of beige across the mirrored top.

Joe bent down and picked up a leather vest decorated with iridescent feathers. "Did we happen on the scene of a struggle?" he asked as he placed it on a hanger. "Or is this the way Ruby always leaves her things?"

"I'd say she left in an awful hurry," Frank

replied. "She didn't even bother to put away her cleaning materials."

He pointed to a little table in the corner. On it were a plastic bottle of laundry bleach, another of ammonia, a metal funnel, and a package of party balloons. The funnel had left a white mark on the tabletop.

Joe studied the collection with mounting excitement. "So she filled one balloon with bleach and another with ammonia, tied the necks shut, and tossed them at us," he said.

"That's what it looks like," Frank replied. "We'd better leave this stuff exactly as it is and find Ruby Bloom. She has a few questions to answer."

Nancy was at the foot of the stairs with Johnny and Kevin. Kevin glared up at Frank and Joe. "Where were—" he began to ask but stopped to answer a question of Johnny's. Joe gave Nancy a significant nod and cast his eyes back up the stairs.

Kevin was now showing Johnny the burst balloons. "My guys found them just here," he explained. "Ammonia and bleach—a nasty mixture. We're lucky no one was blinded, or worse."

"It was thrown straight at me," Johnny said with a shudder. "If Nancy hadn't yelled—"

Joe broke in. "Have any of you seen Ruby Bloom?"

Startled by the abrupt question, Kevin answered quickly, "I saw her leaving the theater a little while ago. She was in a bit of a rush. Why?"

Joe said, "I wanted to check something with her, that's all." Nancy was studying his face. He mouthed the word, "Later," and she nodded.

"I hate this!" Johnny suddenly exclaimed. "This whole place is getting on my nerves. If this keeps up, I'll never be in shape to perform tomorrow."

"Take a break, why don't you?" Kevin suggested. "See something of the city. You're not scheduled to rehearse again today."

Johnny looked thoughtful. "That's not a bad idea. Listen, Nancy, will you let me take you to lunch? Call it a reward for saving me just now. There's a great little place in Montmartre that I've been wanting to try."

Nancy thought for a moment. Lunch with Johnny Crockett at a romantic Parisian restaurant was bound to be a memorable event. It would also be a great opportunity to find out more about him. She might even manage to learn why someone had such a grudge against him that he was willing to risk blinding him.

On the other hand, she didn't want to get *too* intimate with him. The memory of Alan's unhappy face at the café, asking about Bess, flashed into her mind and inspired a solution to her problem.

"That sounds wonderful," she said. "And I'll bet Alan and Bess would love to join us."

Johnny looked cross, but after a brief hesitation he said, "Sure, good idea." He looked at Joe and Frank. "How about you guys?"

"Thanks," Frank replied, "but we'd better pass this time. We have a meeting to attend."

Nancy looked down at her jeans. They were spattered with pale spots from the drops of bleach. "I'll walk you out," she told Joe and Frank. "I have to go over to the hotel to change."

"You tell Bess," Johnny said. "I'll find Alan and meet you in front of the hotel in fifteen minutes."

Johnny turned and walked away. As soon as he was out of hearing, Nancy asked, "What did you find?"

Joe told her about the ammonia and bleach in Ruby's dressing room. "She's obviously the one behind the harassment," he concluded.

"I think she's getting a little help," Nancy said, remembering the scene between Ruby and Roger at the café earlier.

"Isn't it a little too obvious, though?" Frank asked. "If she's the one, would she have left her door open and all the evidence right there in plain sight? Somebody could be trying to pin it on her."

"Maybe," Nancy said thoughtfully. "Or maybe being a superstar has made her think that the rules don't apply to her, that she can do anything she likes and get away with it."

"Hey, you guys," Joe said. He sounded excited. "Come over here and take a look at this."

Joe was standing next to the mailboxes. Each box was labeled with a name. He was pointing to a box near the center of a lower row. The label read B. Peeler.

"B for Bobby?" Joe said softly. "I think we just discovered how Fiona is supposed to get in touch with the Conductor's accomplice."

"I think you're right," Frank replied. "Now the question is, who is he?"

"There's something that bothers me more than that," Nancy said with a frown. "Why was he so easy to find?"

Joe stood in the middle of the courtyard and turned his head to stare. The Louvre museum was four tall stories of time-blackened stone, and each of its two wings was at least as long as four football fields. Along the top story there were niches with life-size statues every thirty feet or so. In the center of the stone-paved courtyard was a strikingly modern pyramid of glass that seemed to float on the surface of the reflecting pools that surrounded it.

Frank took his arm. "Come on," he said. "We don't want to be late." He looked around. "How do you suppose we get in?"

Joe pointed to the glass pyramid. "Well, a lot of people are going into that thing," he said, "and not many are coming out. Either it's the entrance or a people-eating UFO."

Frank slapped him on the shoulder. "Come on, little brother, let's take our chances."

Once they were inside the pyramid, the clear

glass seemed to vanish, leaving only the sky and the delicate lacework of metal supports above them. They walked down a winding staircase to an underground lobby. A guard pointed out the brightly lit tunnel that led to the conference center.

Outside the door to the conference center a man with watchful eyes asked for their passports. "Haven't seen you here before," he said to the brothers, checking off their names on a roster.

"Please wear these in a prominent place," he said, handing them each a plastic nametag with a band of magnetic tape imbedded in it. "For your own protection, you understand."

Inside, they stopped at the bulletin board and studied the afternoon schedule.

"'Indelible Identification Workshop'?" Frank read. "Sounds too technical. How about 'Art Smuggling in Historical Perspective'?"

Joe shook his head. "I'm not that interested in how it used to be done," he said. "I want to know how they're doing it now."

"Techniques haven't changed all that much," said a voice just inches from his ear.

Joe jumped. "I wish you'd stop sneaking up on me, Fiona. It's bad for my nerves."

"I didn't," she protested. "I always walk lightly. It's part of my training." Shifting only her eyes, she checked out the corridor before speaking. "I have to talk to you," she said softly.

Joe double-checked. There was no one within hearing range. "You've had another message from the Conductor?" he asked. Fiona nodded. "Let's see."

"I can't show you," Fiona said, her eyes focused over Joe's shoulder. "I destroyed it. It was much too dangerous."

Frank leaned in. "Dangerous? Why? What was it?"

She hesitated. "A list—of places and dates."

"Places and dates?" Joe repeated. "Of what? Capers you and your father pulled off?"

She glared at him. "Ssh! Some things are better left unsaid."

"Was it accurate?" asked Frank.

She nodded again and gazed at him with eyes that seemed to fill her whole face. "Frighteningly so. Listen, Frank—"

"Ah, the brothers Hardy!" a voice boomed. "I was asking myself when I would see you again."

Flustered at being caught talking to Fiona, they turned to face the portly middle-aged man moving toward them. Frank said, "Oh, hello, Commissaire Guillaume. How are you?"

"Very well," he replied. "And this is Mademoiselle Renardine, is it not? We met at this morning's seminar," he explained to Joe and Frank. "Mademoiselle Renardine made a very interesting point about certain flaws in the alarm systems now being installed in many museums. It is fortunate for us that you are not a professional thief, mademoiselle. You would be far too successful."

Fiona laughed easily. "Thank you, Monsieur le

Commissaire. I hope you can find time to share your thoughts with me about the motion-sensitive systems. However, just now I must dash. If you'll excuse me?"

As Fiona hurried away, Commissaire Guillaume mused, "A fascinating young lady, Mademoiselle Renardine. I am surprised that someone so young is so knowledgeable about security matters. But I beg your pardons! You, too, are young, and your reputation as detectives is well known. Still, it is astonishing."

He continued in a sterner voice, "Have you anything more to tell me about the subject of our conversation yesterday?"

"The Conductor, you mean?" said Frank.

"Exactly. I cannot force you to confide in me, of course. But if you are withholding information that might help prevent a crime—the movement of stolen masterpieces out of my country, for example—the consequences could be extremely serious. I point this out for your own good, and because of my great respect for your father."

"We understand, sir," Joe replied. "And the minute we find out anything definite, we'll tell you."

"That's a promise," Frank added.

"Thank you," the French police official said. "That is what I wanted. Now, I plan to attend a session on the links between art smuggling and organized crime. It should be very interesting. Would you care to join me?"

"Thank you," Joe said after sharing a quick glance and a nod with Frank.

As she stood up from the table, Nancy took a last look out the window. It was hard to believe the view wasn't a picture postcard taped to the wall. The restaurant Johnny had taken them to was in an old building perched on the very edge of Montmartre, the hill that dominated the northern edge of Paris. Over the rooftops of the houses lower down on the steep slope, they could see the whole city laid out before them, from the Eiffel Tower to Notre Dame Cathedral.

"I don't think I can move," Bess groaned when they reached the street. "That dessert I ordered was heavenly. What is it called? The little pastries filled with ice cream and smothered in hot fudge sauce?"

"I think it was profiteroles," Alan replied.

Bess giggled. "There must be a joke in that, but I'm too tired to think of it. What now, gang?"

Johnny, who was hiding from his fans behind a large hat and sunglasses, thumbed through a guidebook. "This street is supposed to be the heart of old Montmartre," he announced. "Why don't we walk up to the top?"

The narrow cobblestone street curved steeply up the hill. They stepped off the sidewalk to ease past a painter and his easel and got an angry blast from a crowded tour bus. If only the tourists knew it was Johnny Crockett the bus was honking out of the way, Nancy thought, and smiled to herself.

Up ahead, Bess and Alan were walking hand in hand. Wasn't this April in Paris, just like the song? She glanced over at Johnny. During lunch she felt she was starting to get to know the real person behind the rock superstar.

Johnny intercepted her glance and misinterpreted it. "There's no place like Paris," he said softly, slipping an arm around Nancy's waist.

Gently but firmly, she removed his hand. "Sorry, I'm here on business," she said just as softly. "Remember?"

"And you never mix business with pleasure," Johnny replied. "I understand." Was he making fun of her? Nancy was sure she saw laughter in his eyes.

Around the next curve Nancy caught the gleam of Sacré-Coeur. Pure white against an azure sky, the church was framed on either side by ancient houses that leaned on one another for support. Take one down and they'd all fall like dominoes. The church had been painted and photographed from every angle by every tourist and artist who ever visited Paris, but Nancy decided that none of them could capture the beauty of the real-life experience.

Johnny noticed her reaction. "Fantastic, isn't it?" Quietly they circled the church, and then Johnny checked his guidebook again. "According to this, there's a railroad car that runs on a track with cable for power. We can ride to the bottom of the hill." He shouted ahead to Bess and Alan, "The station is just down those steps on the right."

They followed Alan and Bess down a stairway that was bordered by trees and had a row of old cast-iron lampposts running through the center of it. The funicular station was one flight down.

While they were paying their fares, one of the small railway cars slid away from the platform and slowly plunged down the steep slope.

"Missed it," Johnny said as they passed through the turnstiles onto the now empty platform.

"We won't have to wait long," Nancy pointed out, leaning over the folding gate at the edge of the platform to stare down the hill. At the bottom an identical car was beginning its journey back up the slope. Nancy thought it was strange that they would walk right into the front of the car. Most trains were boarded from the side. She was looking forward to the ride in the funicular.

Just then Nancy heard the turnstile click twice. She looked over her shoulder. Two men had stepped onto the platform behind them—both were wearing sunglasses and leather jackets. As she watched, one of them pulled a blue bandanna up over his nose, and the other pulled up a red one. They looked like outlaws in a cowboy movie.

One of them moved in on Johnny, grabbing him by the arms and pinning them to his sides. The one in the blue bandanna straight-armed

Nancy. She was lying flat on her back on the platform before she got back her balance to defend herself.

Alan saw what was happening and jumped on the back of Nancy's attacker and began to pound him.

"Okay, Crockett!" the red-bandannaed one shouted. "Where are the disks?"

"Get lost, creep," Johnny answered him. He almost wrenched one arm free and elbowed the guy in the midsection. The thug gasped, but kept his grip on Johnny.

There were shouts from the change booth and from lower down the hill. Nancy glanced quickly around. The second funicular car was almost back up the hill. The conductor was leaning out the window, shaking his fist at them.

Bess had run to help Alan, who was now kicking the one with the blue bandanna in the shins.

Nancy hopped up and saw her opening. She aimed a kick at Johnny's attacker's knees.

He shouted with pain and suddenly released Johnny to clutch his injured knee.

"No!" Bess screamed. "Johnny, look out!"

Off-balance, Johnny fell back against the waist-high folding gate that blocked the open end of the platform. Tumbling over it, he rolled off the platform onto the tracks, straight into the path of the oncoming funicular.

Chapter

Fourteen

FOUR PASSENGERS had their faces pressed against the front window of the car, their eyes wide and their mouths open and screaming. Nancy watched in horror as the steel carriage narrowed the gap to the platform and docked with a solid metallic clang.

Bess was screaming, too, drowning out the change booth attendant, who was shouting into the telephone and gesturing with his free hand.

"I'm outta here," one of the masked men said. He pushed Alan off his partner's back, and the two of them made for the exit gate. Nancy made a grab for the nearest one's bandanna. He wrenched free, but Nancy's nails raked his cheek.

Her heart in her throat, Nancy hopped off the

side of the platform and climbed over the railing and onto the tracks. Ignoring the shouts of the attendant, she dropped to the ground and peered between the wheels of the car into the gloom. She dreaded what she knew she had to see.

"Johnny?" she called out. "Can you hear me?"

Something stirred in the shadows. A moment later she heard a groan.

"Nancy?" Johnny said faintly. "I can't move —there's not enough room. Maybe you could help; you're smaller."

Nancy crawled partway under the car. One sleeve of Johnny's jacket had gotten caught on the underside of the carriage. She tugged it free, and he scooted forward until Alan could grab his feet and pull him out.

"Whew," he said, sitting up. Johnny's face and hands were filthy, his jacket was ripped in two places, and he had a bump coming out on his forehead. Right then, Nancy thought, no one would recognize him as the glamorous rock star Johnny Crockett.

Nancy heard the attendant call down from the platform. "Please do not let him move," he said in broken English. "Help will be here within minutes."

"The police?" Johnny said. He quickly pulled himself to his feet. "We've got to get out of here. I don't need this kind of publicity. Come on!"

He started to clamber up onto the platform.

Nancy exchanged a shrug with Bess and Alan. They didn't have any choice but to follow Johnny.

The attendant shouted, "I insist that you stay!" But he and the three passengers who had been in the car were forced to step aside as Johnny ran past. "My reports!" the attendant shouted. "What shall I say?"

The distinctive sound of a police siren told Nancy that at least one patrol car was close and quickly coming closer.

"Down the stairway," Johnny said. He took the steps three at a time, with Alan close behind. Nancy and Bess had to make do with two at a time.

From the top the stairway stretched forever for Nancy and Bess. By the time they reached the final step their knees ached and their legs were shaky with fatigue.

Johnny was standing with the door of a taxi open. "Get in, quick," he said, then told the driver to take them to the Hôtel de Ville, the Paris city hall. "We can walk from there," he explained under his breath.

Once the taxi was a few blocks from the funicular, everyone relaxed a little. "I was really scared there for a minute," Bess admitted.

"You think *you* were scared," Johnny retorted in such a droll manner that they all laughed. "I was lucky I fell flat between the tracks."

Nancy took a deep breath, let it out slowly, and

143

studied Johnny. However terrifying his experience had been, he was making a quick recovery, Nancy was pleased to see.

"We learned at least one thing back there," Nancy said. "Our two bandit friends are American."

"How do you know?" Alan asked.

Nancy looked at him. "At a time like that who but an American is going to say, 'I'm outta here'?"

"Johnny, what did they want from you?" asked Bess. "What did they say?"

Johnny shrugged, then noticed Nancy's eyes on him. "They said to hand over the disks."

"Disks? What disks?"

"I don't know," Johnny replied, shaking his head. "But I don't think they meant demos of our next monster hit."

Nancy frowned. "I bet they meant the missing computer disks, the ones with the financial records on them."

Alan's gaze moved to Johnny's face. "But why would they come after you? You don't have them, do you?"

"Of course not!" Johnny said indignantly. "Don't be ridiculous!"

"Then why?" Alan continued.

"I can guess," Johnny said. "I have a key to the box the disks are kept in. If the disks were stolen, and there wasn't any sign of a break-in, then it figures they were taken by someone with a key. Right?"

Nancy scrutinized Johnny. Did he have any idea how incriminating his statement was? Why had he volunteered that information about the key? Because he knew it would be still more damaging if someone else found it out?

That didn't answer the question of who the goons were and who had sent them. Nancy was still silent and thinking when the taxi dropped them at the city hall. They walked the few blocks to the hotel, where Johnny left them, saying, "I've got to clean up and rest."

"We all should," said Alan. "Don't forget, the whole tour is getting together at that club on the Left Bank tonight."

Johnny nodded and turned to Nancy. "I'm sorry our afternoon ended the way it did. I hope you won't let it spoil your memory of the rest of it."

"No chance of that," Nancy replied. No chance at all, she added silently.

Nancy, Bess, Frank, and Joe followed Jules through the brightly lit streets of the Latin Quarter, on the Left Bank, dodging streams of students. Jules abruptly turned into a tiny, roughly paved alley lined with tall, tightly shuttered houses. The only light came from old wrought-iron lamps high on the walls.

"Are you sure this is the way?" Bess asked, glancing around nervously.

"Trust me," Jules replied. "I was the one who told Johnny about the place."

A few yards farther along, the alley ended at a blank stone wall.

"I wanted to show you this," said Jules. "It's one of the only pieces left of the old wall that surrounded Paris. Just think, eight hundred years ago, inside here was the city, and on the other side of the wall were thick forests filled with wolves and other wild animals."

"From what I've seen, it hasn't changed that much," Frank remarked.

Nancy nudged him with her elbow. "How do we get to the club?" she asked. "Climb the wall?"

Jules laughed. "Not quite. Follow me." He led them back a few yards to what appeared to be a doorway but was actually a passage through the building. On the far side, it widened into a dim courtyard with a single sad-looking tree in its center.

"These houses are all built on top of the club, which is in the cellar of a monastery from the Middle Ages," Jules explained. "The cellar has stone walls about six feet thick, so it makes a great rock club. You can crank up the volume all you want without bothering the neighbors. Watch your step, the stairs are pretty worn," he explained.

At the bottom of the twisting flight of steps, Jules pounded the knocker on a massive wooden door, then gave his name to a man in a monk's robe, who led them inside.

Nancy stopped in the doorway and drank in

the scene. The walls were huge blocks of stone with thick stone pillars holding up a vaulted ceiling dark from centuries of smoke and dust. On the far side of the room a band in colorful full-length robes played music with an intense North African beat.

Bess grabbed Nancy's arm and pointed, then she waved excitedly. Johnny and Alan were sitting at a big round table just off the dance floor. Johnny saw them and waved back, then gestured to the empty seats on either side of him.

As they made their way through the crowd, Nancy glanced over and caught a sullen expression on Jules's face. He didn't seemed thrilled at the thought of sharing Bess with Alan.

A few minutes later Nancy came back from dancing with Joe to see that Roger and Ruby had taken over a table two away from Johnny's. They were glaring at each other and seemed on the verge of a full-tilt argument.

Ruby noticed Nancy, too, and gave her a very unfriendly look. Was she jealous because Nancy was sitting with Johnny? Or was there some other reason?

The band launched into a dreamy tune full of long tremolo notes. Jules leaned over to Nancy and said, "In France this is called *un slow*. Would you like to try it with me?"

Nancy stood up. "Sure." What better opportunity to ask Jules a few questions? Jules held her close as they moved across the floor. She rested her cheek on his chest for a moment.

"Jules?" Nancy ventured, leaning back to look in his eyes.

"Yes?"

"When you took us to the Eiffel Tower yesterday, you came up, too, didn't you?" she asked.

Jules pulled away abruptly. "What makes you think such a thing?" he demanded.

"I saw you," Nancy replied matter-of-factly. "You were there to give a large manila envelope to a girl with a red guidebook in her hand, weren't you?"

He laughed easily. "Why should I answer your questions? You already know all the answers!"

"Not quite. I don't know *why* you did it."

"What does it matter?" He shrugged. "I was doing someone a favor, that's all. Nothing to do with you or me. Why are you so curious about it?"

Nancy thought furiously and finally said, "The girl with the guidebook is a friend of Joe's and Frank's, and they'd like to know who sent her that envelope."

"Oh," Jules said with laughter in his voice. "Well, if it's that sort of business, Johnny sent it."

Nancy stared up at him in amazement. "*Johnny* asked you to deliver that envelope?"

"Sure, more or less. One of the guys on the crew brought it to me from him."

"And he said he got it from Johnny, personally? Please think back. It's terribly important."

Jules stopped dancing and loosened his hold

on her so he could take a step back. "Was there something wrong with that envelope?" he demanded. "The whole setup seemed pretty strange to me, but in the music business you learn that strange is normal. What's this all about? Some kind of blackmail?"

Nancy blinked in surprise. His guess was too close to the truth—if it was a guess.

"I can't really tell you," she replied. "It's not my secret."

"I get you," Jules said. "Okay, what happened is this. My guy found the envelope, and another envelope addressed to me, in his mailbox. There was a note attached, asking him to get it to me. Which he did. I read my instructions and carried them out. That's it."

Nancy's mind seethed with ideas. "In other words," she said, "as far as you know, that envelope could have come from Johnny or from the man in the moon."

"Now that you put it that way, I guess so," said Jules unhappily. "I can ask Johnny, if you'd like."

"No, don't do that," Nancy replied evenly. Jules gave her a strange look. "He has enough to deal with," Nancy explained. "I can find out some other way, without bothering him."

Their path back to the table took them right past Ruby and Roger. Ruby sprang out of her chair directly into Nancy's path.

"I hear you've been asking questions about me," she said. "Why?"

Nancy started to edge past her, but Ruby grabbed her arm. "No, wait," she said. "I want to tell you a little story. A while back, when Johnny and I were still together, Alan told us how he got his first big break. It was quite a story, complete with gangsters, kidnappers, and record pirates. The stars included his old girlfriend from the sticks and her best friend, an amateur detective. Does that ring any bells, Nancy Drew?"

Jules was staring at Nancy, a confused look on his face. Nancy managed to keep her face expressionless, but inside she was in turmoil. Ruby had just blown her cover, but would it ruin her investigation?

Roger put his hand on Ruby's shoulder, trying to restrain her, but she shrugged him off. "I'd love to catch your act, Nancy Drew," she said sarcastically. "Come on, give us a sample. Why don't you detect something about me?"

"Not right now, thanks," Nancy said politely.

"Aw, go ahead!" Ruby quickly sidestepped to block Nancy again. "You *do* detect things, don't you?"

"Sure," Nancy answered evenly. "I detect that you didn't change clothes before you came here this evening."

"Yeah? What makes you say that?"

"Those bleach stains on your black velvet pants," Nancy replied pointedly. "Even with a funnel, it's hard to pour liquid into a balloon without spilling a little, isn't it?"

Ruby looked down at her pants. Her face was

almost as white as her hair. "I don't know what you're talking about," she whispered.

"Sure you do, Ruby. And if I were you, I'd quit now, before anyone gets really hurt." Nancy leveled her gaze on Roger and added, "I'd make sure that my friends quit, too."

"I think you can count on it," Roger began, but Nancy had stopped listening. Two beefy guys in leather jackets were just leaving the club and took all her attention. One of them had fresh scratches on his cheek.

Nancy hurried back to her table and leaned in toward Frank. "Come on," she said urgently. "We've got work to do." They fell in behind her as she dashed across the dance floor, up the worn stairs, and out into the courtyard.

"Too late," she panted. The courtyard was just as dimly lit as before, but they could all see that it was empty. Nancy took a deep breath, filling her lungs with fresh air, and said, "I don't know how, but they gave us the slip."

"Who?" Joe asked.

"The guys who attacked Johnny today. At least I think so. I also think—"

The rest of her sentence was drowned out by the sudden roar of a powerful engine. To their left, from a darkened doorway across the courtyard, a dazzling beam of light cut a white slash in the cool night air. A motorcycle shot out of a hiding place, aimed for the exit.

Frank ran to intercept it, but his foot slipped on the uneven cobblestones. Nancy watched as his feet flew up and he slammed down, hard, against the rough ground. He forced himself to try to sit up, but he wobbled and fell over again.

The two-cycle engine was gunned and kicked into high gear as it changed course and headed in Frank's direction. The driver had taken dead aim at Frank, and Nancy and Joe were too far away to get to him in time!

Chapter

Fifteen

INSPIRATION HIT NANCY. "Joe!" was the single word she shouted as she lifted the lid off a plastic garbage can. Joe hoisted the can itself and heaved it over Frank's head, straight into the path of the motorcycle. Garbage showered down everywhere.

Nancy whirled, aiming the lid like a discus, and let go.

In the faint light the black plastic lid appeared huge and lethal. The bike tires shrieked as the driver swerved. A stream of sparks shot into the dark as the tailpipe scraped the pavement.

The sudden maneuver unseated the guy behind the driver—who fell on one knee. He ran a few steps, limping back to the bike, where his partner was revving the engine. The two riders roared into the narrow passage and out of sight.

"Ouch," Frank said, standing and rubbing the back of his head. "Did either of you catch the plate number on that bike?"

"The rear lamp was out, and the courtyard was too dim to see it," Joe explained.

"Well, Nan, you sure called it right," Frank continued. "Those must have been the same guys, unless this town is full of people who get their kicks from running down helpless pedestrians."

Joe was staring toward the empty passageway, his body rigid, his hands balled into fists. "Ten seconds earlier," he said. "Just ten seconds, and we'd have had them."

"We'll catch up to them eventually," Nancy said. "Meanwhile, I've got a new problem to deal with." She quickly filled them in on her exchange with Ruby. "So as of this evening, Bess and I no longer have a cover," she concluded.

"Don't be sure of that," Frank said thoughtfully. "Ruby may not tell anyone about you—now that she knows you've found out she and Roger have been harassing Johnny. You know, Nan, your case is really over—Alan asked you to find out who was sabotaging Johnny, and you did."

"Do you think I'd go back on a promise to you guys? We said we'd back each other—we still have to help Fiona by uncovering the Conductor, and we have to figure out if someone is really skimming money from the tour. I'd say my case is only a third over."

"Okay, then, Nancy Drew. You're something special," Frank said quietly, resting his hands on her shoulders.

Nancy didn't know if it was the magic of the night and ancient courtyard or Frank's touch, but she felt suddenly lightheaded and faint. Tearing her eyes from Frank's, she forced herself to retreat down the stairs and back into the club.

After the quiet courtyard, the sound inside hit her like a solid wall.

"Hey, Nancy," Johnny shouted, standing to greet her. "Dance?" he mouthed.

"Sure," Nancy mouthed back.

Dancing with Johnny Crockett should have taken all of Nancy's attention, but her mind kept wandering back to the case, and when Brent Travis strolled into the club, something clicked in Nancy's mind. What if the proceeds of the tour *were* being embezzled, as Roger said? The most likely suspect would be Brent, who was in charge of the tour's finances. And the most likely place to find evidence was on the missing computer disks.

Brent kept saying that the disks didn't matter, but what if he was simply trying to diguise their real importance? Nancy had definitely seen panic on his face when he discovered that they were gone.

"Ground control to Nancy," Johnny said, putting his lips close to her ear. "Are you dazed with happiness or bored out of your gourd?"

"Oh, sorry," Nancy said, blushing. "I just remembered something. Can we go back to the table?"

"Sure."

Halfway across the dance floor Johnny was stopped by a guy with a rugged face and long blond hair, wearing black leather pants and a sleeveless red T-shirt. Johnny excused himself and stopped to talk to the guy as Nancy continued on to the table.

Joe and Frank were there, chatting with one of the tour's sound men. "We have to talk," Nancy told them. "I think I'm on to something. Where's Bess?"

"She and Alan decided to get some fresh air," Joe replied. "They'll be back soon."

"I have to say goodbye to Jules, then let's do the same," Nancy said. "There's bound to be a quiet café nearby where we can talk. There are a couple more things I want to run by you."

After they had been seated at a little café and had ordered, Nancy began by telling the Hardys Jules's story of delivering the envelope to Fiona.

"I always thought Johnny was involved," Frank said.

"Johnny? Frank, you weren't listening. Anyone could have sent that envelope." She stared at him.

"Look, Nancy, you shouldn't let Johnny's

fame or his obvious interest in you warp your judgment. Personal feelings have no place in a proper investigation."

"*I* know that, Frank," she said, not bothering to hide the hurt in her voice. "What I don't know is why you think you need to remind me of it. Are you sure *you're* not letting your judgment be warped? There's no reason to think Johnny's involved. Next I suppose you'll be accusing him of being the Conductor!"

"Now, wait a minute," Joe began. "Aren't we getting a little worked up over this?"

"As a matter of fact," Frank said, ignoring his brother's attempt to cool things down, "I do think Johnny might be the Conductor."

"That's ridiculous!"

"Is it? Who 'probably' sent Jules with that envelope for Fiona? Who on the tour has the ego to think he can take on the police of the whole world and get away with it? Who is probably looking for a new source of thrills, now that he's made it to the top?"

Nancy pushed back her chair and stood up. She decided Frank was jealous of the attention Johnny was paying her and thought it would be better if she left. With great control she said, "We don't know who sent that envelope. As for the rest, all it amounts to is that you don't like Johnny. That's your right, but it doesn't make him a criminal."

Joe put his hand on her arm, urging her to sit

back down. She lifted it off and added, "There's no point in our arguing like this. I'm going back to the hotel. If you see Bess, tell her where I am."

As she walked away to hail a cab, Frank called, "Wait a sec, Nancy," but she pretended not to hear. She was tired and angry, and she wanted to be alone.

Back in her room Nancy lay down with all her clothes on and stared at the ceiling. She knew Frank had to be wrong. Just because Johnny was a rock 'n' roll star, she hadn't lost her perspective about him. Also, she didn't feel that she'd taken her mind off the case for one moment.

She had a lot of respect for the Hardys. They were both top-flight detectives, but Frank's suspicion of Johnny and his distrust of her had ruined the sense of triumph she felt at unmasking Ruby and Roger.

She sat up and looked at her watch. Back in the States it was around six o'clock, dinnertime. Ned Nickerson might be in his dorm room at school. She picked up the phone and dialed.

After long silences and a series of weird electronic noises, she heard Ned answer. Just the sound of his voice lifted her spirits.

"Hi," she said. "It's me."

"Nancy!" Ned cried joyfully. "It's great to hear from you. How's the investigation going?"

"All right," she said.

"You sound down. Is anything wrong?"

Nancy asked herself if she should tell Ned about her problems with Frank. Then she decided, what was the point?

"I miss you," she whispered. As she said it, she realized that she was telling him the simple truth.

"I miss you, too," Ned replied. "Don't get hooked on Paris. I want you to come back here."

"Don't worry," she said. "I'll be home— before you know it. I just wish . . ." Nancy paused. "Uh-oh, there's Bess's key in the lock. I'll see you soon." She blew a kiss into the mouthpiece and hung up.

Bess did a little dance step as she came into the room. "What a fabulous evening," she said. "Alan and I took a long walk along the Seine, then we went to look at Notre Dame by moonlight, then we had a bowl of real onion soup and freshly baked bread in a little bistro. Nancy, I think I'm in love."

"With Alan? What about Jules?"

"Oh, not *them*," Bess replied. Humming to herself, she danced across the room and out onto the balcony. She flung her arms wide and spun back to face Nancy, announcing, "I'm in love with Paris!"

"I'm sorry, Frank," Joe said as they approached their hotel. "I still think you were a little out of line."

"I tried to say I was sorry," Frank retorted. "You saw what happened. She just walked away!

And, anyway, I was only doing it for her own good. I hate to see that guy make a monkey of her."

They had been discussing Frank's argument with Nancy the whole way back to the hotel, and Joe had a strong feeling he wasn't getting anywhere. Frank was suspicious of Johnny Crockett, and the fact that he had practically nothing to back up his suspicions made him more set in his mind.

"Nancy's pretty levelheaded," Joe observed as they entered the lobby. "She'll be okay."

The desk clerk recognized them and had their key ready. He also handed them a slip of paper.

"'We must talk to you at once,'" Frank read. "'Please call the moment you come in.' Signed, F. This sounds serious," he told his brother.

Five minutes later the Hardys were sitting with Fiona and her father in a small lounge off the lobby. Dr. Fox was pale and short of breath. It occurred to Frank that he shouldn't be so suspicious of Fiona. The Foxes may very well have left their life of crime because of Dr. Fox's health.

"We have very little time," Fiona was saying in an undertone. "The Conductor demands that we agree to his plan by midafternoon tomorrow. If we don't, he now says he'll reveal everything he knows about us."

"Why not agree, and then back out later?" Joe asked. "That would buy more time."

Dr. Fox cleared his throat. "In that case," he said, "the consequences would be even worse.

Apparently, he has evidence that would cost us our freedom for many years."

Frank asked, "How are you supposed to let him know your answer?"

"I was told to bring a note for Bobby Peeler to the stage entrance of the Pont Neuf Theater tomorrow, no later than three o'clock."

Joe frowned. "The first performance of the World Hunger concert is tomorrow at three. The place will be mobbed."

"He's probably counting on that as a cover," Frank said. He turned to Fiona. "I think you should do as you were told."

"What?" she gasped, putting her hand to her throat. "But I can't!" She glanced quickly at her father, then added, "We won't go back to that life. We can't!"

"You don't have to," Frank said. "All you have to do is leave a note addressed to Bobby Peeler. Bring it to the stage entrance of the Pont Neuf no later than two forty-five."

He gave her a grim smile. "Don't worry. Joe and I'll be waiting to see who picks it up. We're going to set a little trap to derail the Conductor."

Chapter

Sixteen

As SHE AND BESS entered the hotel dining room the next morning, Nancy noticed all the empty tables and said, "That party must have lasted pretty late last night. Everybody's sleeping in."

"They're resting up for the performance this afternoon," Bess explained. "No one's on call before noon except some of the techies."

Nancy smiled. "You know all about it."

A hint of pink crept into her friend's cheeks. "Well," she said, "between Alan and Jules, I've learned a lot more about the tour. Think of it as research for our investigation."

Nancy smiled and let Bess's comment pass.

There was no point in irritating her friend again with a comment about their investigation.

After they sat down, Nancy ordered tea, and Bess chose hot chocolate. As she selected a croissant from the basket in the center of the table, Bess said, "I'm sure I've put on five pounds in the two days we've been here, and that's not counting desserts. Now I'll have ten pounds to lose instead of five. Oh, well, it's worth it," she said, slathering butter and strawberry preserves on her croissant.

"You look fine to me," Nancy replied. "Now, while you've been doing our 'research,' have you come across any Englishmen in the company?"

"Englishmen? Oh—you mean that note with the word *labours* in it." Bess wrinkled her nose and concentrated. "No, I don't think so," she finally said. "In fact, Alan said something about how this was an all-American tour. Those balloons filled with bleach and ammonia really spooked him, by the way. He said if we can't take care of the harassment before the tour leaves for Rome, the tension may break the company up."

"I think that's all taken care of," Nancy replied. While Bess listened openmouthed, she described the scene with Ruby the night before.

"Then it's been Ruby all along?" Bess demanded when Nancy finished.

"She and Roger," Nancy replied. "The evidence points to Roger as the one who sent the bouquet of nettles and glued Johnny's dressing room door shut. Ruby practically confessed out-

163

right to throwing the bleach and ammonia balloons. My guess is that she had no idea how dangerous it really was."

Bess nodded slowly. "I can see her doing that," she said. "But I don't see her hiring a couple of hoods to beat up Johnny."

"Neither do I," Nancy replied. "I think what's confused us is that we're dealing with more than one case at the same time, involving mostly the same people. Remember, when those thugs attacked Johnny yesterday in Montmartre, they asked him where the disks were?"

"So they weren't just harassing him," Bess reasoned. "They were after something particular, something they thought he had."

"It looks that way. When we finish breakfast, let's go over to the theater and poke around. A lot of things about those missing disks don't add up."

"Great idea, Nancy," Bess replied. "Except—"

"Except what?"

The color in Bess's cheeks deepened to red. "Well, I told Jules I'd go with him to the Beaubourg museum this morning. He said I shouldn't miss it." She glanced at her watch. "He'll be down here any minute."

After a short silence, Bess added, "I'm sorry, Nancy. I know I'm not being as much help as I should. Listen, I'll meet you later at the theater, and I'll do whatever I can then. Okay?"

"Sure, Bess," Nancy said. She glanced up at

the doorway into the dining room. Jules was standing there, two helmets dangling from his hand. She gave him a wave. "There's Jules now," she said.

Bess scrambled to her feet and threw an arm around Nancy in a quick hug.

"Enjoy yourself—I'll see you later," Nancy told her, and then poured another cup of tea. She stirred it for a long time, watching the reflections of the chandelier in the ripples. She couldn't help feeling deserted as the waiter cleared away Bess's plate and cup.

"Hi, Nancy. Can I join you?" Alan pulled out the chair Bess had just vacated and sat down. "Is Bess still asleep?"

"No, she went off to see the Beaubourg," Nancy replied.

Alan's face tensed. "With Jules?"

Nancy nodded.

He shrugged and stared off over his right shoulder.

"Look, Alan—" Nancy began.

"I know, I know. It's been great seeing Bess again, but there's no future in it. When the tour takes off for Rome, you guys go back to River Heights. Is that what you were going to say?"

Nancy nodded sympathetically. "Something like that."

"I do know all that; it's hard to remember."

"I can tell you one thing, though. She'll remember her moonlight walk with you through Paris last night for a long time."

Alan slouched back in his chair. "So will I," he said softly. "That's something, I guess."

They sat quietly for a few minutes, each staring into the space over the other's shoulder. Finally Nancy broke the silence. "Do you know if anybody on the tour is English?"

"Back to detecting?" he said, grinning at her. "Nope, no Brits. Johnny recruited everyone from talent to techies in L.A. We're American as apple pie à la mode."

"*A la mode* is French," Nancy joked. Then a thought crossed her mind. "Hey, but what about Jules? He's part of the tour, and he's French."

"Oh, he was," Alan said. "But not anymore. He's been living in L.A. for years."

Nancy held back a sigh of exasperation. "Let me put my question another way," she said. "Do you know of anybody on the tour who was born in England, Scotland, Ireland, Wales, New Zealand, or Australia?"

Alan laughed out loud and shook his head. "I don't think so. Except maybe—"

"Mademoiselle Drew?" the waiter said. "Excuse me for interrupting, but you have a telephone call. You may take it in the lobby."

"Oh, thank you. Alan, I'll be right back."

She followed the waiter to the lobby, where he directed her to a telephone in a tiny alcove. She picked up the old-fashioned receiver and said, "Hello?"

"Hi, Nancy, it's Joe. Listen, there've been

some important developments." Nancy listened as Joe told her about the message Fiona had received and the trap that he and Frank were planning to set for the Conductor.

"The Conductor?" Nancy asked when he was finished. "You mean Johnny Crockett, according to your brother."

"Look," Joe replied, "Frank felt really awful about your argument afterward. Why don't we all give it a rest? With any luck we'll know by dinnertime who the Conductor really is."

"You're right. Let's get together right away and talk strategy. Meet you in the café behind the theater in ten minutes."

"Sure. See you then."

When Nancy returned to the dining room, her table was empty. Alan must have gotten tired of waiting and left. She shrugged it off but made a mental note to look him up later.

Nancy made a quick detour to her room for her jacket. The sun was shining, but the air seemed cooler than it had the day before.

The Hardys were already at the café when she arrived. She slipped into the chair between them and gave each of them a smile. "So this is our big day," she remarked. "The day we discover who the Conductor is."

"We hope so," Joe said, "but you know the saying about counting your chickens."

"Not to mention the one about a bird in the hand," Frank added with a chuckle.

Nancy felt the tension in her shoulders start to drain away. Things were going to be okay between Frank and her again.

"Now, about this afternoon," Frank said. "Here's one way we might work it. . . ."

Frank had been talking for several minutes when he glanced up and then fell silent. Johnny Crockett was crossing the street in their direction.

"Hi, gang," Johnny said in a loud voice, almost as if he hoped to be overheard. "Beautiful day, isn't it?"

Not waiting for an invitation, he pulled out the fourth chair and sat down. Leaning his elbows on the table, he spoke very softly but intently.

"Listen, I don't have much time," he explained. "Someone just phoned me in my room. He told me that unless I want things to get worse, I have to come to the base of the bronze column in the middle of the place de la Bastille right away."

"It could be some kind of trap," Joe said.

"I *know* that," Johnny replied through clenched teeth. "But maybe we can turn the trap on whoever these guys are if we act fast. Why don't you take a cab to the place de la Bastille right now? I'll come in about five minutes. They'll probably be watching for somebody to follow me, but I don't think they'll expect someone to come ahead of me."

Frank looked over at Nancy and Joe, then

nodded. "You're on. It's a pretty big open area, though. How can we be sure to link up?"

"There's the new opera house on the far side. You can't miss it. Ask your driver to let you off right in front of it. Now, get going—somebody might be watching me."

He leaned back in his chair and said out loud, "Complimentary tickets for this afternoon's show? Sure, no problem. I'll leave them at the box office."

"Thanks," Frank replied, just as loudly. He, Joe, and Nancy stood up and sauntered away. When an empty taxi came along just moments later, they climbed in.

"Is Johnny for real?" Joe demanded. "Is he being brave, stupid, or crooked?"

"Or are we the stupid ones?" Frank asked quietly. "Maybe he's sending us on a wild-goose chase while he gets set up back at the theater."

"We'll know soon enough," Nancy said, deciding not to confront Frank. "I think that's the place de la Bastille just ahead."

They peered straight ahead through the windshield at a tall, greenish bronze column. The gilded statue at the top glittered in the sunlight. At the foot of the column was a small circular building of white stone.

"We drove by here before," Joe remarked. "I remember this crazy traffic."

Their driver saw his chance and darted into the steady stream of cars circling the *place* even on a

169

Sunday. Halfway around, he slowed down, then darted through more traffic to stop at the curb.

"The new Opéra," he announced.

Johnny was right. The building was unmistakable. Light and dark gray, with huge expanses of glass, the new opera house looked like an ocean liner that had gone badly off course and beached in the middle of Paris.

"Now we make like tourists," Frank said, popping out and craning his neck to look at the building.

"That's easy, we are tourists," Nancy pointed out. "Is Johnny really supposed to go over to the base of the column? With this traffic, he'll be run over in five seconds."

"Look," Joe said, "there's Johnny now, in that cab that just pulled up."

The rock star got out, looked around, and stepped out onto the pavement. A car honked loudly, another barely missed him, but he kept walking.

"There's the answer to your question, Nan," Joe announced. "Look at him. The guy is definitely not playing with a full deck!"

Unconsciously they all held their breath as Johnny waded into the main stream of cars. But the traffic parted around him, and moments later Johnny was standing on the sidewalk next to the circular stone base of the column. He looked up at the column, then began to circle it to his left.

"Come on," Frank said urgently. "We can't lose him now!"

As they started across the wide expanse of pavement, Frank knew there had to be a system to the traffic lights. At one moment the cars came at them from one angle, and a moment later from a different angle. Finally the cars were brought to a stop by two converging lines of traffic. Frank suddenly shouted, "Now!"

They dashed across the momentarily empty pavement to the concrete island that housed the column.

"Now to find Johnny," Nancy said softly.

"That shouldn't be hard," said Frank. "It's not a very big area."

They stopped after they had gone a little over halfway around. "Well?" Nancy demanded. "Where is he?"

"Either he crossed to the other side of the *place* without our seeing him," said Frank, "or he's inside the column. Look, there's a door."

An iron fence surrounded the base of the column. Joe tugged open a rusty gate, and they hurried through. At first the door in the base refused to budge, but finally it squealed in protest and swung open.

Stepping inside, they found themselves in a high-domed chamber. No one else was there. The dim light revealed a stairway that rose up inside the column.

"He must have gone up," Joe whispered. "Let's go."

"Wait," Frank said. "Listen."

From somewhere they heard angry voices.

Frank tiptoed around the room and stopped beside a grille set low into the wall. He pointed at it after beckoning Joe and Nancy to his side.

The voices sounded louder and clearer, and they were shouting. Frank reached down and pulled on the metal. It swung open. He met the eyes of the others and shot them an alarmed glance.

The shouting below them was suddenly cut off by a loud splash.

Nancy uttered a soft cry.

"Help, help!" came a shout from below them.

Frank recognized the voice as that of Johnny Crockett, loved by millions of fans worldwide.

Then there was only silence.

Chapter

Seventeen

"Hurry!" Frank shouted. "The stairs must go down, too!"

He ducked through a low doorway and clattered down a flight of metal stairs, with Nancy and Joe close behind. The echoes of their footfalls bounced back at them from crazy, dizzying angles.

They were descending into a gloomy tunnel, a quarter filled with a river of water. The stairs ended at a narrow stone footpath, a single bank to the water that cast oily reflections on the walls in the dim light.

"There he is!" Joe exclaimed, stripping off his jacket and loafers. He dived into the water and swam a couple of strokes to the center of a circle of expanding ripples. Then he jackknifed and disappeared under the water.

Frank held his breath for what seemed like a minute. When Joe at last reappeared he was swimming one-handed to the footpath, his other hand dragging a body. Frank and Nancy knelt down on the slimy stones and stretched out their hands to help him.

"Here, take him," Joe gasped. As he pushed Johnny toward them, the rock star began to sputter and thrash around. "Hey, easy!" Joe said in his ear. "We're friends."

Frank and Nancy grabbed Johnny under the arms and hauled him up onto the path. For a few moments he lay on his back, panting. Then suddenly he sat up and started coughing. Joe hoisted himself out of the water, stripped off his shirt, and started to wring it out.

"Thanks, guys," Johnny choked out. "I was already seeing my obituary in the fan magazines."

"What happened?" Nancy demanded.

"Two big guys were waiting for me. The same ones as yesterday—I think." He stopped and coughed. "They hustled me down here and told me to hand over the disks or else. When I said I didn't have them, they tossed me in and ran off. I must have hit my head because I'm a good swimmer usually."

Johnny looked around the tunnel. In one direction it stretched off into deeper gloom. In the other direction not very far off was a circle of daylight.

"This must be the canal!" Nancy exclaimed. Frank's expression was puzzled.

"You remember," she continued. "The one Jules talked about the other day. He told us that it ran under the place de la Bastille."

"Jules, huh?" Frank said. "I wonder how many other people on the tour know about this place?"

"Probably not too many," Nancy said. "Our two goons must have escaped down the canal in a boat. They were well prepared."

"Hey," Joe said, "can we talk about it later, after Johnny and I get into some dry clothes? I'm freezing!"

Once out in the open again, they flagged down a taxi. The driver wasn't happy about taking two soaking-wet passengers, but Frank and Nancy spread their jackets on the seat to keep it dry, and Johnny promised him a big tip.

In front of the hotel again Johnny sat in the cab for a minute to catch his breath before pushing through the fans, who always hung out in front. He kissed Nancy on both cheeks. "I owe all of you one," he said. "Come on, Joe, I'll give you a dry set of clothes."

"I'll meet you two over at the café as soon as I change," Joe said, following Johnny as he pushed his way in the front entrance.

Frank and Nancy walked over to the café and sat in their usual spot.

"Conference time," Frank announced. "We have a few unsolved mysteries to deal with. Number one, who's sending those two hoods, or are they on their own?"

"I'm willing to bet it's Brent," Nancy said. "He's desperate to get those disks back because maybe they can prove he's been embezzling money from the tour. And Brent's convinced Johnny has them because he has the only other key to the box."

Frank raised his eyes and studied the passing clouds for a moment, then said, "Okay, let's say it's Brent. It's still just a theory, but if it's true, where does it lead us? What about Johnny? Does he have the disks? And if he doesn't, who does?"

Nancy shook her head. "You got me."

"My turn, then," Frank continued. "I don't see any sign that Johnny has them. If he did, why would he keep quiet about it? He wants this tour to make money to help world hunger. Why would he allow Brent to skim money? It makes no sense—he's involved, too."

"He could be planning to blackmail Brent," Nancy said. She didn't sound very convinced.

"He could be," said Frank, "but what would he gain by doing that? He'd come out further ahead by exposing him. Nope, I vote that Johnny doesn't have them."

"Then who does?"

Frank gave a French-style shrug. "Beats me," he said. "Maybe they really were destroyed in the fire."

Nancy pulled a scratch pad and pen from her purse and began to doodle. "Hmm," she said. "Maybe."

"Let's move on to our next mystery," Frank said. "Who's—"

"Oh, look. Here's the answer to one mystery already solved," Nancy said with a nod.

"Huh?" Frank said. Roger Hart, in dark glasses and a big hat, was strolling across the street. "I see your point," Frank said. "Wouldn't you hate to be a rock star and have to wear disguises all the time?"

"Mind if I join you for a minute?" Roger asked. He sat down before they nodded and continued. "Was Ruby right about you guys being detectives?"

"Why do you want to know?" Frank asked.

Roger leaned forward to answer, but his elbow knocked a spoon off the table. He bent down to retrieve it, and when he surfaced again, he was red-faced.

"Well," he said hesitantly, "it's not hard to guess why you're here. It has to be the—uh, 'practical' jokes. And, well, I just want to say that you might as well go home. There won't be any more jokes played on Johnny. That's all over now."

"Oh?" said Nancy. "Why?"

"Maybe it was getting out of hand," he replied. "Sometimes people do things without thinking or without realizing how dangerous they might be. And sometimes they find out that the things they were upset about aren't as serious as they thought."

Frank studied Roger's face. He sensed the rocker had come as close to confessing as he was going to.

"Are you saying we should just forget the whole thing?" Frank demanded.

Roger nodded. "For the good of the tour, yes. But don't just take my word. Ask Johnny what he thinks. He and I had a long talk at the club last night about the way he's been running things. I think he's going to take other people's feelings into account more. He's even decided to open this afternoon's show himself. And after today we'll use a rotation system to decide on the order of the acts."

"Sorry I took so long," Joe said, pulling out a chair and sitting down. "You would not believe how many times I had to wash my hair. Hi, Roger, what's new?"

"This and that," Roger replied, getting to his feet. "Frank and Nancy can fill you in. I've got to get back to the theater. Wish me luck getting through those fans."

"What was that about?" Joe asked as Roger walked away.

"He more or less confessed to pulling those practical jokes," Frank explained. "He also promised there wouldn't be any more of them."

"You know," Nancy said, "I think I saw him laying down the law to Ruby last night. That must be why she got so mad and came at me like that."

"Well, there you go," Joe said. "Your case is solved. Now it's on to the Conductor. And if everything goes as planned, we'll wrap that one up in a few hours."

"I don't know what it is," Nancy said, "but something's been bothering me. I don't like the way this guy is acting. It makes no sense."

"Which guy?" asked Frank.

"The Conductor." The top sheet of her pad was full of doodles. She tore it off and went on to the next page.

"Let's say you're a top smuggler and you want to send an important and secret message to a top burglar," she continued. "How do you do it?"

Frank frowned. "You'd probably do it in an ordinary way so that no one would notice—like sending a letter or dropping it by the other guy's house. Something like that."

"Exactly," Nancy replied. "What you *don't* do is force your burglar to go all the way to the top of the Eiffel Tower, then arrange for someone else to be sent to deliver an obviously mysterious envelope to your burglar there!"

"You're right, it makes no sense," Joe said. "It's as if the Conductor wants to be noticed."

Frank leaned forward eagerly. "Now that you mention it, what about all those messages he keeps sending to Fiona? What's the point of them? They just increase the risk of detection for both of them. The guy must be a total flake."

"That isn't his reputation," Nancy pointed out, tapping her pen. "He's supposed to be the best. What do you make of that?"

"You know," Joe began, "every single thing we know about the Conductor comes from the same source—Fiona. How far should we—"

He broke off in midsentence. Kevin was striding down the sidewalk toward them.

"Hello, hello," he said, stopping next to the table. "I hear we owe you three some thanks."

"You saw Johnny?" Frank asked.

"Yeah, just now." He pulled out a chair and plopped down, setting his shoulder bag on the pavement next to his chair. "I don't mind telling you that I feel a bit put out about all this. After all, I'm supposed to be in charge of security around here. Having one of my stars attacked and nearly drowned doesn't add to my reputation, does it?"

Joe laughed. "No, I guess not," he said.

"Mind you, it's not really my fault," Kevin continued. "Johnny slips away from his bodyguards all the time. It's like a game with him, so what can I do?"

He glanced down at his feet, then bent over. When he sat up, he had a pencil in his hand. "Does this belong to any of you?"

They shook their heads.

"Ah, well," he said, sticking it in his shirt pocket, "waste not, want not. I'm off. I have a thousand things to do, and I've got to get back to the theater by two. See you later."

After he left Frank said, "It's noon. We'd better eat some lunch and make sure we make it back to the theater by two forty-five."

"Good idea," Nancy said. She reached down for her purse, but it wasn't under the chair. After groping for a moment, she took a look and found it under the table. She must have kicked it, she decided.

Nancy grabbed the strap with her fingers and slid the purse toward her. As she did something slipped out and fell to the pavement.

"What?" She jumped up and circled the table to pick up a small manila envelope, about six inches by nine inches. There was no address, no mark of any sort on it. She knew she'd never seen it before.

"What's that?" Frank asked.

"I think somebody gave us a little present," Nancy said.

She reached into the envelope. Then her eyes went wide as she pulled out what was inside. Clutched in her hand were a half-dozen computer disks.

Chapter

Eighteen

FRANK AND JOE examined the disks with her. Three of them were labeled "Accounts—WHR Tour" and numbered one through three. The others were simply marked *A*, *B*, and *C*.

Frank pointed at the lettered disks. "Backup?" he said.

"If they're backup, wouldn't they be labeled?" Joe asked.

"Good point," Nancy said.

"Three and three," Frank mused. "What if they're two different versions of the same thing?"

Joe raised an eyebrow. "Two sets of books? You mean, one for people to see and one that really shows where the money went?"

"Why not?" Frank replied. "It happens all the time."

Nancy slipped the disks back into the envelope and tucked it into her purse. "Brent was frightened when he discovered the disks were missing," she pointed out. "Why would he be scared if they were simply the accounts and backups? He told me that his office in the States has copies of the tour accounts. So these must have something different on them."

"Too bad we can't read them without a computer," Joe said. "I wonder if Commissaire Guillaume could help us."

Frank nodded. "We'll have to give him a try. But what I want to know is, who put the disks in Nancy's purse and why?"

"Good question," Joe said. "Nancy, who's been close enough to you this morning to have done it?"

"Well—Alan and Johnny and Roger and Kevin, and, of course, you two, and Bess. And the waiter."

Frank concentrated. "Let's see if we can't narrow it down. When did you last look into your purse?"

"I took some money out for the cab," Nancy said hesitantly. "Wait! After we sat down, remember? I was looking for a pen and paper. If the envelope had been there, I'm sure I would have noticed it."

"Roger!" Frank exclaimed. "Sure! Remember when he knocked the spoon off the table? He must have done it on purpose so he could slip the disks into your purse. And all that stuff about giving up his campaign against Johnny was a lie. He's been saying all along that Johnny's a crook. He must think the proof is on the disks."

Joe looked skeptical. "If he had the proof in his hands, why didn't he just give us the disks? Why stick them in Nancy's purse?"

"Maybe he thought the proof would look better coming from a detective," Frank suggested. "Or maybe he was afraid Johnny's friends and fans would resent it if they knew he was responsible."

Joe still looked skeptical. "But how did he manage to take the disks?"

Frank shrugged. "Maybe Brent left the office open one time. Or maybe there are more keys around than Brent knows about."

Nancy stared at him. "You mean, somebody like the head of security might have one?" she said.

"Kevin? Of course, but why would he want to steal the disks and then slip them to you?"

"I have no idea," Nancy replied. "But he was in a better position to steal them than Roger. And when he was here, he ducked under the table to pick up a pencil. A yellow pencil on a gray sidewalk is hard to miss. Did either of you notice it before?"

"Nope," Frank said, and Joe shook his head.

"Neither did I. Maybe because it wasn't there.

He could have pretended to pick it up while he was putting the envelope in my purse."

"Okay, you've got opportunity," Joe said, "but no motive. With Roger, we've got both."

"I don't know," Nancy mused. "Maybe Kevin is really committed to fighting world hunger, and it makes him mad to think that the money is lining somebody's pocket instead. So when we showed up, and he discovered we were detectives, he decided to get the evidence and turn it over to us."

"Nice try," Joe said, shaking his head, "but I don't think that theory hangs together. Why couldn't he simply hand us the disks and tell us what was on them?"

"Good question," Nancy admitted. "But maybe Frank's right, too. Maybe he's afraid to jeopardize his career. After all, tour managers might think twice about hiring a security chief who steals things, even if it is for a good cause."

"Or maybe he has something to hide and can't risk the publicity," Joe added.

Frank cleared his throat. "Well, whatever his motive—if his *is* the one—it looks as if we've recovered the missing disks.

"We won't know for sure until we get to a computer," Nancy said. "And that'll have to wait until after the concert. Right now we've got to concentrate on the big one, the Conductor. Are we pretty positive that he's connected with the World Hunger Rock Tour?"

"Everything points that way," Frank replied.

Nancy frowned in concentration. "With any luck, we'll find out *who* he is this afternoon. But meanwhile, we don't know *how* he's doing it."

Frank looked at her in confusion. "Doing what?"

"Smuggling stolen paintings out of Paris," Nancy said.

"We already talked about that," Joe said. "He crosses the border with the tour."

"I know," Nancy said, "but where are the paintings? This is a rock tour, not a traveling art gallery. What does he do with the art? We're talking about fragile pieces of canvas that are worth millions of dollars. He can't risk losing or damaging them. So where does he put them to keep them safe *and* hidden?"

Joe shrugged. "In something, I guess. A box of some kind or a crate—"

Nancy shook her head. "Some curious customs man might come along, open it, and say, 'Well, what have we here?' No, it has to be something much less suspicious."

Frank stared at the theater. He suddenly slapped his forehead with his palm. "Of course!" he exclaimed. "Come on, you guys, we have work to do!" He tossed some money on the table and strode away from the café.

"Where are we going?" Joe asked as he and Nancy followed Frank across the street toward the stage entrance of the theater.

Over his shoulder Frank gave them a triumphant grin. "We're going to look at a few instrument cases," he replied.

It took them several minutes to find the right storeroom just behind the stage, and several more for Joe to pick the lock. As they stepped inside and clicked on the light, they gasped.

"A few instrument cases?" Joe repeated.

Cases for guitars, amps, keyboards, and drums were stacked high, all the way around the room.

"This is hopeless," Joe said. "We'll never be able to look through all these."

"Right," Frank retorted. "And a customs agent who opens the doors of the truck that carries all this stuff is going to say the same thing. He might look into one or two, but more likely he'll just wave the truck through. But we have an advantage over him. We know what we're looking for."

"I don't get it. What help is that?" Joe asked.

"I think I see what you mean," Nancy said, looking around the room. "Unless the Conductor takes the paintings off their stretchers, which could damage or even destroy them, he has to hide them in something that's big enough. So we can cross at least half of these cases off the list right away."

"That's how it looks to me," Frank agreed. "Some of the guitar cases might do, but I think the keyboard cases are the most likely suspects."

"Oh, boy," Joe said. "I count about ten of them, and they're at the bottom of the pile. We'll have to shift all the other cases to get to them, and the longer we're in here, the more likely it is that someone will find us."

Frank was intently studying stacks of cases. "Hey," he said, "am I right that Johnny's band uses only two keyboards?"

Nancy frowned, concentrating. "You're right," she finally said.

"Then why do I see *three* keyboard cases marked 'Johnny Crockett Band'?"

Joe said, "Maybe he carries a spare."

"Maybe," Frank replied. "Let's find out."

The first two cases they opened were empty. The third contained a synthesizer. "See?" Joe said. "Like I said—a spare."

"I guess you were right," Frank said, dejected.

"Good try," Nancy said, reaching down to close the case. "Hey," she said, her tone of voice changing. "Doesn't this lid seem a lot thicker than the others?"

Frank knelt down to the instrument case and felt the inside of the lid. "It sure does," he said. "I'd say there's about an inch and a half unaccounted for."

Frank began to push, pull, and turn every screw and fitting on the lid, first one by one, then two at a time. "We must be wrong," he said finally. "Maybe it's just extra padding or—"

Click!

A plush-covered panel fell forward, revealing two padded compartments concealed in the lid. One of them was empty. But the other—

"Wow!" Nancy exclaimed. She reached down

and carefully removed a canvas stretched on a wooden framework from the case, then turned it around.

A pair of acrobats, father and son, solemnly stared back at them. The background, their costumes, even their skin, were all in different and subtle shades of blue. Nancy, Joe, and Frank studied the canvas in silence.

"It's a Picasso," Nancy said breathlessly.

"It is," Frank said in a hushed voice. "From his Blue Period. We saw a photo of it in the paper a couple of days ago. And guess what?" He paused.

"It's the one that was stolen from the Delatour Collection!"

Chapter

Nineteen

INCREDIBLE!" NANCY EXCLAIMED. "We've actually recovered one of the stolen paintings!"

"It's fantastic," Joe agreed, "but a little scary, too. We can't keep a lid on something this big. What do we do?"

"We've got to bring in the authorities," Frank said. He pulled out Commissaire Guillaume's card with his private telephone number. "I'm going to give the commissaire a call."

"Good idea," Nancy said. "We'll stay here and guard the painting. Signal us when you come back—two knocks, then one. And hurry," she added. "If the Conductor finds us here . . ." She purposely left her sentence unfinished.

Frank nodded, then disappeared. After about

five minutes Nancy and Joe heard the signal on the door. Nancy turned the lock and pulled the door just wide enough to let Frank slip back inside the storage room.

"I finally got through to Guillaume," he said in an undertone. "He couldn't believe what we'd done at first. The French police have been searching the whole country for the Delatour Picassos. He said he'll be here in"—he glanced at his watch—"seven and a half minutes."

"Great," Nancy said, then frowned. "But how is he going to keep from alerting the Conductor? If a bunch of police officers come tearing in here, our guy is going to know that something's up. And if you ask me, catching him is at least as important as recovering the painting. If he stays in circulation, a lot more great paintings are going to turn up missing."

"Good point, Nancy," Frank replied, "but I thought of that. Guillaume said he'll pretend to be making a last-minute check of the security arrangements for this afternoon's concert. Apparently, there are a lot of different police authorities in France, so no one will think twice about another one getting in on the act."

Frank glanced at his watch again. "I'm going to go wait near the stage entrance for the commissaire. Unless he ran into a traffic jam, he should be here right about now."

He slipped out the door, and Joe locked it behind him. Only a few moments later Frank tapped on the door once more.

Commissaire Guillaume had brought two officers with him. One of them went over to the canvas and picked it up reverently. Handling it gingerly, he held it at arm's length, then peered at certain parts with his nose almost touching the canvas. Finally he looked over at the commissaire and nodded silently.

"Formidable!" Guillaume exclaimed. He met Nancy's eyes. "You must be Mademoiselle Drew," he said. "You and my young Hardy friends have performed a great service for France. No, for the whole world!"

Then his tone changed. "However, after my investigators have completed their work here, I believe we should all return to my office. You must see that this discovery of yours raises a great many difficult questions. I hope you have good answers."

"The Conductor, eh?" Guillaume said. Joe, Frank, and Nancy were in his office in an ancient stone building that overlooked the Seine. They had just finished telling him about their investigation.

The police official swiveled his chair around so that it faced the window and its view of the river. His elbows rested on the arms of his chair, and he held his hands near his face with the fingertips pressed together.

"I thought that he might have some role in this affair," he continued. "The question is, how can

192

we unmask him and recover the second Picasso?"

"Well, sir," Frank said, clearing his throat. "We have a plan. It's not very elaborate, but so far the Conductor doesn't know we're after him. He may not be on guard against a trap."

Guillaume revolved his chair so that he was looking straight at the three detectives. "A trap? Tell me more, my friend."

Frank glanced at Joe and Nancy, then continued. "The Conductor expects an accomplice of his to bring an important message to the theater at two forty-five. The message will be addressed to a false name the Conductor uses. We are going to be waiting near the mailboxes to see who picks up the note."

Guillaume heaved a sigh. "Well, it's worth a try," he said finally. "I will have men outside the theater and backstage, if you need assistance."

Nancy said, "Won't it alarm the Conductor if a lot of police suddenly show up?"

The commissaire chuckled. "No problem, my dear young lady. We shall simply say that we have had word of a possible security problem and wish to provide extra protection for the distinguished artists from America. Shall we go?"

Joe had a sudden flash of inspiration. "Well, there's something else, sir," he said. He quickly explained about the computer disks and what he thought might be on them. "I don't know if there's enough time now, but—"

"No problem, my dear young friend," he said. He reached for the telephone, dialed three numbers, and then spoke in rapid French to the person at the other end of the line.

"We are in luck," he reported when he hung up. "Monsieur Lortic, one of the Sûreté's best experts on business and computer fraud, is in his office today. He has invited us to join him there."

Joe, Frank, and Nancy followed Commissaire Guillaume down the hall and up a flight of stairs to a door that was ajar.

"Please come in," Monsieur Lortic called. He was much younger than Guillaume, perhaps thirty, and had a round, cheerful face. They entered, and the commissaire introduced them.

Joe looked around curiously. Wooden bookcases, jammed with big, dusty leatherbound books, lined one wall. Along the opposite wall was a long table on which sat two computers and a remote terminal. The window behind Lortic's desk looked out into a stone-paved courtyard that probably hadn't changed since the Middle Ages. It was hard for Joe to imagine a setting more filled with contrasts.

For the next half-hour he stood in the background with Frank and Nancy while Monsieur Lortic worked first to get the data from the computer disks to his screen, then to make sense of the parading columns of numbers. Joe was beginning to wonder if they would get back to the theater in time. Still, he sensed that there was no way to hurry the accounting expert.

Finally Lortic pushed his chair back from the computer and said, "It will take much more time to unravel all this."

Disappointed, Joe said, "You mean the disks don't—"

Lortic held up his hand. "To be quite sure, in a legal sense, is complex. But there are indications—"

"Indications of what, monsieur?" asked Nancy.

"The tour has regularly been transferring important sums, hundreds of thousands of dollars, to a corporation headquartered in one of the smaller independent countries in the West Indies. A country that is well known for its lack of curiosity about the companies that have their headquarters there. There is no sign of what, if anything, the corporation has done to earn such payments. In my opinion, this pattern is one that cries out for further investigation."

Joe exchanged a triumphant look with Nancy and Frank. "In other words," he said, "someone's been siphoning off money. Embezzling it."

Lortic nodded slowly. "It looks that way. If I confirm my initial impression, the person responsible will be in serious trouble."

"I'm sorry," Frank said. He had just looked at his watch. "We've got to get back to the theater. We're running out of time. Thank you for your help, monsieur."

"No, no," Lortic replied with a smile. "Thank *you* for letting me in on such an interesting case."

"Come," Commissaire Guillaume said. "I'll have you outside the theater in five minutes."

Apparently, Guillaume had forgotten about the opening performance by the World Hunger Rock troupe. Five minutes later the car was sitting in a traffic jam that showed no sign of ever moving again.

"I think we'd better walk," Frank said urgently. "It's almost time."

They climbed out and joined the stream of pedestrians, most of them young, flowing in the direction of the Pont Neuf Theater.

Suddenly Nancy said, "Oh, no!"

"What is it?"

"The passes!"

"Don't worry," Frank said. "I have them right here."

"Not for us. For Fiona!" Nancy exclaimed. "How is she going to get through to the stage door to pass her note?" She looked at Frank questioningly.

Frank stopped so quickly that three people bumped into him. He muttered an apology and started walking again.

"We never thought of that. There goes our plan—shot full of holes."

"Hold on," Joe said. "Okay, so we never thought of it. But what about the Conductor? Why didn't *he* think of it?"

"Good question," Nancy replied. "Maybe he's got too much to handle and just forgot?"

"Maybe," Joe said. "But this guy is a world-class pro. He didn't get that way by forgetting crucial details. My guess is that, for some reason we don't know about, it's not a problem."

Nancy gave a wry grin. "I see what you mean. After all, Fiona is a world-class pro at getting into any place she isn't supposed to. I say we go ahead with the plan. If it works, terrific. If it doesn't, we'll think of something else."

"We won't be allowed to," Frank said. "If we don't catch the Conductor this afternoon, Guillaume will be mounting a full-scale search by nightfall. He can't risk letting the other Picasso slip through his fingers."

"That's right," Nancy said. "And once the Conductor sees all those cops around, he'll go underground. What happens to Fiona then? He'll probably blow the whistle on her and her dad."

"She's depending on us to keep that from happening," Frank said. "She trusts us. Come on!"

The street leading to the stage entrance was blocked off at both ends, but Nancy and the Hardys knew the guard on duty, and they were allowed right in. Nancy glanced at her watch; it was two thirty-seven when they walked backstage.

The theater was transformed. From the auditorium beyond the curtain came the steady hum of thousands of voices. Backstage there seemed to be two sorts of people, those who were rushing around on the edge of panic, and those who were standing in place as if frozen by the thought that the concert was about to start. Nancy, Frank, and Joe found spots in sight of the mailboxes and joined the group that was frozen in place.

At two forty-three the stage door swung open again. Framed by dust-filled sunlight, Fiona paused for an instant, then stepped inside. The door swung closed behind her. She stepped in and handed a white envelope to the guard, who made some sort of joke as he put it in one of the cubbyholes. Her teeth flashed in laughter, then she turned away.

"Hey, Fiona," someone called. "How's it going?"

The girl turned with a startled expression on her face, then hurried off. Nancy was just as startled. The person who had called out to her was Jules. Nancy strolled over to where he was standing. "Who was that?" she asked casually. "A friend of yours?"

"Fiona? Not really," he answered. "I've seen her around. She has friends on the tour."

Nancy swallowed, hoping to keep calm, and glanced to her left. Frank was standing next to her with a grim look on his face. Joe was just behind him.

"I know I've met her somewhere," Nancy said, "but I can't put my finger on it. Who is she friends with?"

"Kevin, I think. They've known each other for many years—from back home." Jules saw her blank stare and added, "I never asked, but I think she's also English."

"Kevin is English?" Frank demanded.

Jules smiled. "He used to be. Now, like me, he's from California. You're surprised? He's done better than me to sound American, perhaps. Excuse me, it's time."

Jules walked over to the wings, where Johnny's guitar was waiting, and picked it up. Nancy, Frank, and Joe stood where he had left them, wordless.

There was no time to talk. At that moment Johnny came from his dressing room. He winked at Nancy as he passed, then paused for an instant next to the mailboxes. Nancy's heart raced with expectation and fear. More than anything, she didn't want to find out that Johnny Crockett was the Conductor.

He crossed over to Jules and strapped on his guitar, then walked onstage, where the band was waiting. Nancy blinked a haze from her eyes and stared at the mailboxes, then she sighed with relief. Fiona's note was still there.

A buzzer sounded. The band struck an ear-bending chord as the red velvet curtain rose. The crowd went crazy when they saw Johnny onstage. Even over the clamor, however, Nancy could hear the opening run of "Set on You."

The audience recognized the song and

screamed even louder. The mood of hysteria spread backstage. Everyone pressed forward to get a better view. Nancy, jostled, backed away from the stage and glanced toward the mailboxes. Then she froze.

Fiona's note was gone!

Chapter

Twenty

NANCY, FRANK, and Joe converged on the mailboxes and stared helplessly. There was no mistake. The cubbyhole labeled B. Peeler was empty.

From onstage, music roared from the speaker towers. Joe leaned close to Frank and Nancy to make himself heard. "I don't get it," he said, pounding his fist into his palm. "How could we have all missed him?"

"The psychological moment," Nancy replied. "When the crowd erupted like that, you would have had to be a robot not to look. The Conductor must have known that and waited for it."

"Then he knew about the trap?" Joe demanded.

"Not necessarily," said Frank. "He may have simply been taking precautions. You don't get to the top of your profession by being careless."

"So what now?" Joe said. "Do we go out and tell Commissaire Guillaume that we blew it?"

"Not quite yet," said Nancy. "Don't forget what Jules told us about Kevin's being English."

Frank whistled softly. "Kevin?" he said. "The Conductor?"

"Maybe. But we need proof."

"There's Jules," Joe said, pointing toward the wings. Twenty or more people were bunched together, watching the show. Jules and Bess were at the back of the crowd. Jules was standing close behind Bess with his hands on her shoulders.

Joe caught their eyes and beckoned them over.

"What is it?" Bess asked as they drew near. "You've found out something, haven't you?"

"All of you look very serious," Jules added. "Is anything wrong?"

"Maybe," Nancy said. "Jules, are you sure about what you told us, that Kevin and Fiona are friends?"

"Kevin and Fiona!" Bess exclaimed, staring in confusion.

"*Friends* is not perhaps exactly the correct word," Jules said. "She came to see him when the tour was in London, I think, and a couple of times since we got here, that is all. They seem more like people who have worked together than friends of the heart."

"Of course," Frank muttered under his breath. How could he have let Fiona fool him so thoroughly?

Joe's voice bubbled with suppressed excitement as he said, "Have you known Kevin a long time?"

"Oh, yes," Jules replied. "More or less. His house in L.A. is not far from mine, but he's always on the road, mostly with international tours. Any American group that is planning a European tour tries to get Kevin for security because he knows the European scene so well. He is one hundred percent professional."

"He certainly seems to be," Nancy said grimly.

"Thanks, Jules," Joe added. "You've helped a lot."

Jules walked back to his spot in the wings. Bess followed him with her eyes, then looked back at the others.

"What's going on?" she demanded. "Is Kevin—"

"Of course," Nancy said. "The Conductor! All this time we've been thinking about train conductors and band conductors. But in rock everyone plays electric instruments, right?"

"Right," Joe said. "So what?"

"So what about *electrical* conductors? Do you remember what you learned about them in physics class?"

"Sure," Frank said. "Electrical conductors are mostly metals, and the best of them are gold, silver, and copper. That's why electrical cords are made of copper."

"Uh-huh," Nancy said. "But what about Bobby Peeler? Did you know that both *bobby* and *peeler* are British slang words for a police officer? Well, who's the head of security, the top police officer of the tour? Kevin, that's who."

"Oh, no!" Bess exclaimed. "I just thought of something else. People call police officers *coppers.*"

Joe stared from Nancy to Bess and back again "You guys are weird," he announced.

"I agree with Joe," Frank said. "You're really reaching."

"Maybe we are, at that," Nancy said with a shake of her head. "It doesn't really matter, though. What counts is that we think we know who the Conductor is. Now we have to find proof."

"You know what?" Frank said. "If Kevin's the Conductor, it explains why he took those disks from Brent's office and passed them on to us. All the talk about embezzlement must have been directing too much attention to the company, which would make his smuggling even harder than usual. He wanted to use our investigation to ease things up for him."

"Are you *sure* he's the Conductor?" Joe asked. "I'm not a hundred percent convinced. Okay, he's English, he's a friend of Fiona's, and he tours a lot. That doesn't make him an art smuggler."

Bess said, "Why don't we just go find him and ask him some questions? If he's in the clear, fine. And if he's not, we can tell Frank and Joe's friend at the Sûreté about him and let the police take it from there."

"Good idea," said Frank. "Let's go."

"I've been keeping an eye out for him while we've been talking," Nancy announced. "He's not here. Why don't we try the dressing rooms?"

The hallway that served the stars' dressing rooms was empty. At the corner they glanced down the corridor that led behind the stage. Kevin was just coming out of the storeroom. His face was gray, and his hands kept clenching and unclenching at his sides.

"He must have just checked on the painting and discovered that it was gone," Nancy whispered.

Turning toward them, he searched their faces with his eyes. For a brief moment his face blazed with anger. Joe recognized the desperation in that glance. Kevin had been found out and he knew it.

Then, without a single word, Kevin wheeled around and sprinted down the corridor.

"Let's go!" Joe cried. "He can't get away with Guillaume's men around the building."

"Sure he can," Nancy said, trailing Joe along the hallway. "He's head of security for the tour, remember? He can come and go as he likes."

As they rounded the corner that ran along a

passage that ran along the far side of the stage, they saw Kevin shouldering one of the fire exits open. The door swung out to reveal a police officer in a blue uniform and white belt standing there.

Kevin quickly pulled the door shut. Glancing back at his pursuers, he seemed to be estimating his chances of barreling his way through them. Without warning, he leapt for the narrow ladder that led up to the fly space above the stage.

"I'll head him off on the other side," Joe said, taking off the way they had come. First Nancy, then Frank, made a dash for the ladder and began to climb. Kevin was already near the top.

The next time Nancy raised her eyes, he had vanished. She forced her arms and legs to move faster.

The heavy curtain that surrounded the stage had muffled the sound of the rock concert, but when she reached the top of the ladder, she was above the curtains. The heavily amplified sound was like an invisible wall that she had to break through to step onto the far catwalk. Frank took the one closer to the wall, five feet from her.

She glanced down, then closed her eyes and swallowed. Johnny and his band were just below her—forty feet down. There was nothing between her and them but two feeble-looking planks and a lot of empty space.

Laser beams darted back and forth. Brilliant strobes flashed in syncopated patterns. The fog machines along the back of the stage were blasting full tilt. Nancy squeezed her eyes shut and clutched at the rope handrail with both fists.

"I'm *not* going to give up," she said to herself. She could barely hear her words over the pressure of the music.

She opened her eyes and tried to peer through the clouds of artificial smoke as she stepped forward. Frank was paralleling her. But where was Kevin?

Nancy caught her breath. She spotted the security head halfway across the expanse of the stage. He wasn't on a catwalk. He was making his way on the connecting two-inch steel pipes from which the lights were hung. Above his head he grasped bundles of power cords to help keep his balance.

Nancy was amazed that he hadn't fallen. The pipes appeared to be strong enough to hold his weight, but the smooth, round surfaces had to be incredibly slippery.

Nancy choked back a scream as Kevin's foot slipped. For a moment that seemed endless, he struggled to regain his balance. Then he was stepping across the pipes again, aiming for the catwalk that Nancy was on. She hurried toward him. From the corner of her eye she saw that Frank, on the neighboring catwalk, was also closing in on him.

The next instant Nancy felt her toe catch on a

rope that was tied around the planks of her catwalk. As she fell forward, the stage spun in a dizzying spiral. She tightened her grip on the rope handrail and hung on desperately.

Then her feet plunged off the catwalk, and Nancy was dangling over a forty-foot drop.

Chapter
Twenty-One

HER GRASP HELD, but as the rope burned into Nancy's fingers, she felt them weakening. She couldn't scream for help because nobody would hear her over the amplified sound of Johnny and his band. One quick glance down confirmed her worst fears, and she quickly shifted her gaze upward.

The planks of the catwalk were pressing against her back, just above her waist. Somehow she had to pull herself back onto the board.

Desperately Nancy pulled, trying to chin herself on the rope, but the rope only stretched down to meet her chin. How much longer could it take the strain of her weight? How much longer could she hold on?

Forty feet below her, Johnny finished his song. The audience burst into cheers and applause.

As the noise died away Nancy yelled, "Help! Help!"

From somewhere nearby, Frank answered her, "Hang on, Nan, I'm coming!"

Nancy almost lost her grip as the catwalk swayed violently under her weight. Then two strong hands were clasping her under the armpits.

"I can't lift you all the way from this angle," Frank said in her ear. "If I take your weight, can you manage to get your foot on the catwalk?"

She nodded but didn't answer. She needed every bit of breath she had.

As Frank's grip tightened and he started to lift her, she twisted at the waist and stretched her right leg as high as she could. Her toes touched the edge of the catwalk, then slipped off.

"Once more," Frank panted. "You almost had it. One, two—"

He lifted her again. Desperately she stretched her leg, groping for the wooden walkway. There it was! She felt it! As she pushed her foot onto it, it touched something rigid. She risked a quick look. It was one of the iron rods that held up the handrope. With a sudden effort, she hooked her foot around it.

"Great!" Frank exclaimed. "Now roll onto—" The rest of his instructions were drowned out by the opening chords of another song.

Nancy's arms felt as if they were being torn

from their sockets. Sweat poured down her fore-head and ran into her eyes. It was now or never. She counted to herself, up to three, took a deep breath, and put every bit of strength she had left into a desperate lunge upward.

Then she was lying full length on the catwalk floor, panting to catch her breath. Frank, kneeling next to her, appeared to be near the end of his reserves, too.

"All right?" he mouthed as the music filled the space around them.

She nodded weakly, then pushed herself up a little to look around. "Kevin?" she mouthed.

Frank pointed to the far end of the catwalk. The message was clear. The Conductor had gotten away from them. Again.

Joe shaded his eyes against the intense glare of the stage lights and stared upward. He was starting to worry. Where was Kevin? And what had happened to Nancy and Frank?

What should he do—stay where he was in the wings or go over to the stage door to alert the police?

From somewhere high above the stage, Joe heard what sounded like a shout, but a line of narrow curtains blocked his view. He moved to one side and continued to stare.

Suddenly someone grabbed his arm. He spun around.

"Joe, there he is!" Bess exclaimed. "Quick! He's getting away!"

Joe saw the flash of a red ponytail moving in the direction of the stage entrance. Joe bore down, dodging the spectators and the stacks of equipment being readied for the next act.

Kevin must have seen Joe coming because he broke into a run. In another minute he'd reach the street. Commissaire Guillaume's police might stop him, but Kevin could slip past.

Joe couldn't take that chance. He launched himself into a flying tackle and connected. Kevin went sprawling. By the time they had recovered from the impact, Commissaire Guillaume and two of his officers were standing over them.

"Felicitations," the police official said to Joe and Bess as his officers cuffed Kevin. "But where are your brother and Mademoiselle Drew?"

"I'm wondering that myself," Joe said. "I think I'd better—"

"Here we are," a familiar voice said.

Startled, Joe raised his head. Frank was slowly climbing down a narrow ladder a few feet away, with Nancy just above him.

As the police were getting ready to take him away, Kevin swiveled his head to look at Nancy. "Do you mind telling me where I slipped up?" he asked.

"You shouldn't have gone for the blackmail," Nancy replied. "When you try to force people to do things, they react in unpredictable ways."

"Blackmail?" he said, perplexed and then angry. "I'm no blackmailer. I—"

The officers were tugging at his arm to move him toward the door as the music erupted again.

As they started away, Kevin shouted something, but Nancy couldn't make out a word over the sound of Roger Hart's latest big hit.

One of the police officers opened the stage door, letting in a dust-laden shaft of brilliant sunlight, and Kevin Fuller, the Conductor and Bobby Peeler, was led away to jail.

Commissaire Guillaume paused long enough to say, "We have also taken Monsieur Travis and his two 'friends' into custody on embezzlement charges. You will be pleased to hear that he has agreed to cooperate. The rest of the proceeds from the tour will go to feed the hungry after all."

"Why did his two goons lock us in that dressing room?" Joe asked his brother.

"I think we were about to stumble on them, and they just reacted," Frank explained.

Nancy barely heard what was being said. She was standing in a daze, staring at the door. A loud warning bell had just gone off in her mind. She had seen something earlier that she desperately needed to recall. She knew it was somehow terribly important. But what?

"Bess, Frank, Joe," she said as the image formed in her mind. "Fiona didn't leave!"

"What?" Frank said. "I don't understand."

"When she came in to leave the note," Nancy explained. "She opened the door, and it shut behind her. She handed the guard the note and turned away. But the door didn't open again. I

213

would have seen the daylight. She stayed back-stage!"

"Okay. So?" Joe asked.

Nancy felt the words and sentences piling up in her mind, too quickly for her tongue to keep up.

"Don't you see? Kevin wasn't blackmailing her and her father at all. All those notes and messages were phony. They were already working together. In fact, I bet the Foxes stole the two Picassos last week. But when she saw you and Frank at the hotel, she cooked up a scheme to get you hunting Kevin. Even if you didn't find him, you'd be kept occupied trying."

"But why?" Joe asked. "Why would they double-cross their own partner like that?"

"The temptation was probably too great," Nancy replied. "They probably figured they could smuggle the two paintings out without Kevin's help and keep the millions for themselves."

"*Two* paintings," Frank repeated. "But we found only one in the instrument case."

"I know. Maybe—"

Nancy's body went rigid. A boy of about sixteen was walking toward the stagedoor. He wore his red hair pulled back in a ponytail. Under his arm he was carrying a large black artist's portfolio.

Nancy narrowed her eyes, then called out. "Not so fast, Fiona!"

With amazing speed, the thief darted toward

the door. A uniformed police officer lunged at her, but she twisted out of his grasp. As Fiona neared the door, she raised her hand to push it open. The portfolio fell to the floor with a crash.

Fiona paused for one split second. She seemed to be debating whether to bend down and pick it up. But the police officer was reaching for her again. That must have decided her. She slammed the door open with her shoulder and dashed out.

"Stop her!" the police officer shouted to the other police blocking the end of the street. But before they could react, Fiona had darted past and disappeared into the crowd.

"I can't believe she got away," Frank said. "She sure made a monkey out of me this time."

"Me, too," Joe said. "I was really feeling sorry for her and her dad."

"Maybe you ought to feel sorry for them," Nancy said. "Fiona may have escaped, but look what she left behind."

Nancy unzipped the black portfolio and pulled out the second of the missing Picassos.

"Hey, everybody," Alan said from behind Nancy. He had come offstage at that minute. He was mopping his face with a towel. "Hi, Bess. How'd you like our set?"

"Fantastic," Bess replied. "But—"

Before she could say any more, Alan noticed the painting in Nancy's hands. "Hey!" he exclaimed. "That's really great! Do you know the artist or something? I'd love to have one like it myself."

Late that Sunday night an old canal boat was moored on the Seine just downstream from the theater. Its owner, an old friend of Jules, had strung colorful paper lanterns above the deck. Near the door to the cabin was a table loaded with peasant breads, a dozen kinds of cheese, pâté, and luscious-looking pastries.

Nancy sat on the railing at the stern, watching the rising moon pave a path of light across the water. The party was fun, and she liked practically everyone she'd met, but she was starting to feel crowded. She need space and a little quiet.

Bess came out on deck and walked over to her. "Oh, Nancy, thank heavens I found you," she said. "I was just standing inside and thinking. You know, I don't know who sent those two thugs after Johnny and who put the note in your suitcase the first day we were here."

"Brent Travis is guilty on both counts. He overheard Johnny and Alan talking about asking us to investigate the practical jokes. He must have gotten scared that we'd uncover his embezzling while we checked out the pranks, so he tried to scare us off. He really did think Johnny had the disks so *he* sent the goons for them," she finished.

Alan, who had been listening to Nancy's explanation, slipped an arm around Bess's shoulders and asked a question, too. "What about the fire? Who set that?"

"I can take that one—Kevin. Right, Nan?" Bess asked.

Nancy nodded. "He didn't think it would be discovered so fast and hoped it would burn the case the disks had been in. That way his theft would be covered up, and Brent wouldn't know that anyone had the disks. Kevin must have figured that if we got too close to him, he'd publish the disks and turn our attention away from him. It was kind of like insurance," Nancy said, completing the explanation.

"Why did Fiona steal her own note?" Bess asked as another question occurred to her.

"To complete the charade. She's a perfectionist," Nancy answered.

"Well, all I can say is, I'm glad it's over," Alan said. "Now we can concentrate on rock 'n' roll. Speaking of music, come on, Bess. They're playing our song."

"But we don't have a song," Bess protested.

"We do now," he replied. As they walked off, arm in arm, he gave Nancy a wink.

After a little time alone, Nancy wandered into the main cabin. Joe was talking to Ruby, who was still cool toward her. He looked up and grinned as she passed.

Nancy found Frank with the boat's owner, who was giving him a short history of the vessel.

"Hi, I was looking for you," Frank said. "Are you okay? You look a little sad."

"I'm okay," Nancy replied. "I'm sorry to be

leaving, that's all. Joe said you'll be here a few more days."

"That's right," Frank said with a smile. "We're finally going to be able to attend our conference. Guillaume wanted to put together a special session about the Conductor, but I talked him out of it." He shook his head slowly. "I still can't believe we let Fiona and her dad walk away like that. It's only thanks to you that they didn't take the other Picasso with them."

"Not me," Nancy said. "Luck."

Across the cabin Johnny Crockett climbed onto a bench and held up his arms for silence.

"Don't worry, guys," he said, "no speeches tonight." Cheers sounded from around the cabin.

He laughed, then continued. "I just want to ask you to give a big hand to Nancy, Joe, Frank, and Bess for saving the reputation of our tour and making it possible for us to do what we set out to do. Let's hear it!"

Everybody clapped and cheered, and someone contributed a piercing whistle. Nancy felt a flush start at her neck and work its way up her cheeks. Was this what Johnny felt when he walked on-stage? If so, it was no wonder that he loved rock 'n' roll.

The applause died down. Jules handed Johnny an acoustic guitar. As he fastened the strap, Johnny found Nancy in the crowd and gave her a roguish look. Unamplified, the notes sounded different, but she could never mistake that opening.

She moved closer, a smile on her face. This was her moment, her real reward. Johnny's gaze was soulful.

Behind the romantic look, though, Nancy detected a hint of laughter as the rock star began to sing, "Set on You."